Airship Daedalus

Legend of the Savage Isle

By Todd Downing

FIRST EDITION

ISBN: 979-8-9861181-0-9

Copyright © 2019 Todd Downing & Deep7 Press

All Rights Reserved Worldwide

Edited by Dan Heinrich & Andrea Edelman

Sensitivity readers Devielle Johnson & C.A. Suleiman

Cover art & design by Todd Downing
(*Daedalus* model by Hans Piwenitzky)

Based on the *Airship Daedalus* / *AEGIS Tales* setting and characters by Todd Downing and published in various media by Deep7 Press. *Airship Daedalus™* and *AEGIS Tales™* are trademarks of Deep7 Press.

WWW.AIRSHIPDAEDALUS.COM

Deep7 Press is a subsidiary of Despot Media, LLC
1214 Woods Rd SE Port Orchard, WA 98366 USA
WWW.DEEP7.COM

To my awesome editorial team
Dan & Andrea,
who make me look good.

And to my intrepid readers,
A toast—to the end of empires.

- PRELUDE -

Paris, August, 1920

The device was the size of a rugby ball, egg-shaped and gray gunmetal whose edges gleamed in the dim light of the chamber. A dozen of Crowley's handpicked acolytes in the Astrum Argentum gathered around the dais, watching with interest as a man in shirt-sleeves and a mechanic's apron made some final adjustments to the object sitting in its center. The man was a German of slight build, with the severe "high fade" haircut favored by soldiers of the Central Powers during the Great War. His bespectacled, boyish face was pale and displayed a well-trimmed triangular mustache and sunken blue eyes. The leather apron he wore covered a starched gray shirt with sleeves neatly rolled to the elbows, and black uniform *jodhpur* breeches met with polished black officer's boots at his knees.

The man secured the device by way of an aluminum clamp housing which somewhat resembled an Art Deco bear trap, splitting the oval face itself into two halves that now lay open to the stone ceiling at 45-degree angles. Furtively scanning the room and finding Crowley in the westernmost point of the chamber, the man blotted at his forehead with a handkerchief and nodded at his master.

"The device is ready," he said cautiously.

"Proceed," said Crowley, showing no emotion in his gaze. His Thelemic priest's robes disguised the trim body of a man in his mid forties, fresh from mountaineering in the eastern United States. His razor-shaved head was a flawless dome, save for a noticeable pit in his left cheek, and his famously color-changing hazel eyes were beginning to sink into fleshy sockets—a consequence of overindulgence in heroin and sex.

The mousy officer in the apron retreated to a doorway opposite Crowley and returned arm in arm with another robed figure, this one even smaller than he. As they approached, the almost-skeletal hands of a crone drew back the crimson hood covering her face, revealing the blank stare of a blind Russian woman, her visage lined and carved in the trials and hardships of life. She was perhaps sixty, but looked half again older, with ash gray hair sprouting in an unruly shock from her tiny, withered skull.

The small officer walked her to the dais and patted her arm softly, indicating she was where she should be. He then ducked to the base of the pedestal and retrieved a small box bristling with toggle switches and a wire running up to the open device. He stood back and addressed the old woman in soft tones.

"Madame Balanovskaya," he said, "you may begin."

The woman's milk-white eyes gazed upon the cold tile floor of the Abbey of Thelema, and a guttural rumble began low in her throat. As the onlookers found themselves stepping backward, flat against the walls of the ritual chamber, Madame Balanovskaya suddenly snapped her head toward the ceiling. Her reed-thin arms shot out from her shoulders, palms upward, and the rumble in her throat now seemed to dislodge from her body and echo throughout the abbey of its own accord. The sound swirled, orbiting the central dais like a edge of a spinning top. The pitch increased, and the sound began to thrum with a steady rhythm.

The atmospheric pressure within the room suddenly increased, and for a moment, it felt like the abbey would break apart from its foundation. But it was the air above the device on the pedestal which cracked open. Like a thunderstorm in miniature, a roiling, billowing cloud of ectoplasmic membrane appeared, sending fingers of lightning down to test the surfaces below. The low thrum became a pitched whine.

As Crowley watched, the first spindly, arachnid-like leg probed out of the roiling storm and extended down to the small platform at the center of the dais, where the egg-shaped device sat open. A second leg, then third, then a fourth followed. And then the horrible face of something designed by forces not of any benign galaxy. The spidery creature crouched upon the platform beneath the tiny lightning storm, dog-sized and shimmering in a jet-black, salamander-like skin. Its claws dug into the stone altar, holding itself in place.

Its eyes opened—all four of them—aglow with eldritch fire, scanning the room intently. Madame Balanovskaya collapsed in a crumpled heap of robes and bony aged flesh. The small officer in the apron almost dropped the switch box to go to her aid, but the creature on the altar had not yet fed. He knew perfect timing was essential.

And feed it did. A drooling maw full of spiny barbs sucked open where its chest should have been, and every head in the room began to swim—all save Aleister Crowley, the unconscious Madame Balanovskaya, and the young Silver Star officer crouched below the creature's line of sight. The sound pulsing through the room became even higher-pitched, and the tiny thunderstorm above the abomination crackled with renewed intensity. Suddenly the room was awash in an unearthly crimson glow. One by one, the onlookers fell, their very life force extracted in beams of ethereal light, terrified screams echoing throughout the abbey as their souls were ripped from them.

When the last acolyte had collapsed into a dead heap, the young officer peered over the top of the altar to see that the creature was in a good position, and flipped the main toggle that deployed the device below. There was a brief shriek as the demon folded in on itself and the two halves of the device snapped shut with a sharp echo.

The thunderstorm dissipated into the shadowy corners of the chamber, and the sound gradually faded away to an ominous silence.

The young officer glanced over the large, oblong demon trap, noting with satisfaction that it was glowing an angry red-purple color. He squatted down to check on the old woman, who was thankfully still alive. He hoped she still had another ritual or two in her. The Astrum Argentum would most likely have to search elsewhere for summoners who could take them beyond the experimental phase of the project.

"Well?" asked the hooded figure at the western point of the circular chamber.

"The ritual was successful, my Master." The bespectacled officer produced an electric motor the size of a typewriter from a small crate next to the dais, and as Crowley observed, began to run wires from the rugby ball device to the battery contacts on the motor, tightening them down with wing nuts. Reaching into his apron pocket, he brought forth a small alkaline battery with wires already taped to the contact points and ending in a twisted length of copper.

Watching closely, the young officer touched the bare wire of the battery to a contact point on the back of the device, and an unholy shriek erupted from within. Immediately the motor revved to life, rotors spinning faster and faster until smoke began to erupt from its insides, finally dying in a shower of sparks and haze.

"We will need to work on a capacitor system to keep overloads like this from happening in the field," the officer told Crowley. "But as you can see, just one nominal 1.5 volt stimulus yielded enough power to do this..." he gestured at the charred remains of the motor. "And no doubt much more."

"Very well," Crowley nodded, turning toward the chamber exit. "You may continue the program." At the door, he stopped, glancing down at the dead body of a former student. Looking back at the officer, he added, "See to this. And tell no one, my dear Mister Himmler. The Infernal Machine is our secret."

- CHAPTER 1 -

Kenya, May, 1927

Jack McGraw squinted through the bridge windscreen canopy as the *Daedalus* made her approach over Nairobi. The capital city, the colonial jewel of British East Africa, bustled with commercial air traffic and commerce of all kinds, but what drew Jack's attention were the half dozen plumes of smoke wafting up from the tribal lands beyond. At full speed, they'd make Mombasa in just over two hours, where their new mechanic awaited them. But these smoke columns were more than a little worrisome. They seemed to straddle the rail line from Nairobi to Mombasa, and seemed too scattered to be the type of controlled burns used to clear farmland or flush game.

A hot morning sun painted the occupants of the airship in golden tones, illuminating the American flying ace-turned-adventurer in his early thirties, square-jawed and blue-eyed, with a crop of copper-tinged blond hair that kept falling in his face. He was badly in need of a trim and a shave. Jack wore a white cotton work shirt, his navy blue trousers sporting a gold stripe down each side, standard issue to all flight officers in the AEGIS Aeronautics Division. The trouser legs disappeared into a pair of shiny black officer's boots that worked the lateral turn controls at his feet. His jaw circled in a chewing motion, working a piece of licorice-flavored Black Jack chewing gum. He always kept a pack on hand, gnawing on a piece whenever he flew, or found himself under stress, or needed to think.

April had been a heck of a month, beginning with their mission to recover the Dagger of Lir from a Celtic crypt beneath the craggy soil on the isle of Scarba. That had quickly become an ambush and running firefight with agents of the Silver Star, which in turn became a tracer-blazing dogfight into the eye of a storm, and the discovery of a super-carrier named *Osiris*, which had the capacity to launch a squadron of six fighter planes from her enormous dirigible frame. Limping to an airfield in southern England, the *Daedalus* crew made repairs, and received a visit from their former comms officer, Edward "Duke" Willis, who had been promoted into command of his own AEGIS LR-3 airship, the *Percival*.

When they made contact with Colonel Stephen Shaw, their handler in London, he'd notified them that the *Percival* had gone missing somewhere over Europe. A frantic search—and several battles—from Rome to Athens to Cairo finally shook loose the right intelligence, which took the *Daedalus* crew to a lost city on the Nile, buried in generations of desert sand. There, in a sunken temple several meters below the desert floor, Maria Blutig, She-Wolf of the Astrum Argentum, was already engaged in a demonic summoning ritual. The blood she was using had once flowed through the veins of the *Percival*'s crew. One by one, she slit their throats, until only Duke remained, ready to die for his crewmates and for the good of humanity that AEGIS represented. Fortunately, Jack, Doc, and the Cherokee sharpshooter known as "Deadeye", had intervened in the temple, as a larger battle raged in the desert canyon above. Maria Blutig was vanquished, for the time being anyway, and the Silver Star was sent packing.

The dark army led by Aleister Crowley had lost the battle, but they'd still come out ahead on two counts: First, they'd managed to extract one of the Edison-DiMarco dynamo generators from the *Percival*'s engine room; secondly, they'd captured Carl "Rivets" Holloway, erstwhile mechanic aboard the *Daedalus*, and arguably the man with the most practical knowledge of AEGIS technology in the world— even more than founder Thomas Edison himself.

In the end, the AEGIS forces had succeeded in retrieving the *Percival* and her commander, but lost vital technology and the man who best knew how to use it. And of course Duke would forever carry the horror of his crewmembers' dying trauma with him.

Jack frowned. It must have been absolute hell. But then, anytime Maria Blutig was involved, "absolute hell" was most often the theme of the party. At that moment, the *Percival* was departing Cairo with a new crew and a rendezvous course to Mombasa, and all Jack could think of was that the sooner they were in pursuit of those who had stolen their technology and, worse, abducted Rivets, the better.

Over Jack's left shoulder sat the comm station, occupied by Lieutenant Marissa Singh, Punjabi linguist and expert in codes. Those very skills had earned her the call sign "Cipher" during her aviation training in England. She stared anxiously out the same forward view ports, gently brushing a stray lock of raven black hair under the band of her red uniform beret, revealing a small ruby-like *bindi* on her forehead. She, too, wore the standard white work shirt, navy trousers, and black boots of an AEGIS Aeronautics officer. Just twenty-five, Cipher was a product of empire, and in recent weeks had come to see some tarnish on her previously unblemished worldview.

Opposite the comms, behind Jack's right shoulder, was navigation. Dorothy "Doc" Starr sat there, her gaze shifting between the forward view ports and her map of East Africa. She was around Jack's age, a fellow veteran of the Great War, and arguably the architect of the covert field service within the Allied Enterprise Group for International Security. She was clad identically to Jack and Cipher, minus the latter's beret, but with the addition of a small crystal shard hanging from her neck on a leather thong. With catlike green eyes, natural walnut-brown curls, and a sly smile, Starr resembled the young Hollywood actress Myrna Loy, who had actually been cast to play her in the movies.

Standing over the back of the pilot's seat between the nav and comms stations, a young Egyptian soldier, Asim, followed his captain's gaze out over the native lands beneath them, running a tan hand across a bristly jaw. The newest recruit to the *Daedalus* crew, Asim had proved his skill as a driver during a deadly car chase through the streets of Cairo just a week and a half ago. Jack saw in the young man an innate spatial awareness and synergy with the machine he drove—specifically, a war-era Crossley troop truck—and thought he might be groomed to fly. Every day since his induction into AEGIS, Asim had taken duty watches in the pilot's seat, picking up some of Jack's tips and tricks, and even some mannerisms. He drew the line at the licorice chewing gum, however.

Their course followed the railroad. To the east lay the expanse of the Taru Desert. To the west, the sprawling lands of the Kikuyu people, and the rising smoke.

"Darn peculiar," Jack muttered.

Doc leaned forward over the nav console, straining to see more. "What do you think it is?"

"It's not spread over a large area," Jack shrugged. "Each column is pretty localized."

"If those are villages," Asim noted, "this could be evidence of a tribal war."

Doc frowned. "This is all Kikuyu territory," she said. "Why would they be fighting each other?"

"It could be an invading force," Asim shrugged.

The words hung hollow in the air. In this part of the world, "invading force" could mean anything from a rival tribe to a colonizing army from Europe. But the *Daedalus* was down one generator and the crew had yet to meet up with the new mechanic, and Jack decided it was probably unwise to venture too close to the source of the smoke. They had their orders, and couldn't let themselves get bogged down in local trouble. He throttled forward to full speed and made for the airfield at Mombasa.

As they passed over the rail town of Voi, however, Jack saw chaos erupting beneath them. The train station was ablaze, a bucket brigade of locals ushering water from a giant tank nearby. Automobiles were flipped upside-down like dead insects in the street. British locals and natives ran in every direction, as the staccato *pop pop pop* of gunfire erupted above the screams of civilians. The corpses of people and animals alike lay baking in the morning sun like a tray of some horrible confection.

"What the—?" Jack felt the *Daedalus* buck slightly as she was impacted from below.

Asim turned to the hatchway that divided the bridge from the rest of the ship. An access door led to the nose turret, which was equipped with quad-mounted Lewis machine guns. "I'll take a look," he said.

The airship banked and veered off to the right, toward a tenant farm nearby.

Jack keyed the *TALK* button on his electric console as he throttled down and spun the *Daedalus* around her nose to get a better look below. "Deadeye? How's it looking up top?"

A burst of static, followed by "All clear topside, Cap," was all that came through.

"Okay, Charlie, why don't you come down here and stand ready with your rifle."

"Affirmative."

Several small pings of metal-on-metal echoed through the airship's envelope, and Doc muttered under her breath, "I know that sound." She stepped gracefully down to peer over Jack's shoulder for a clearer view.

Jack nodded. "Someone's shooting at us."

Another burst of static came over the comms and Asim exclaimed from the nose turret, "Someone's shooting at us!"

"Cipher," Jack ordered, "patch me through to the external loudspeaker."

Cipher flipped a couple switches on her console, and turned back to her captain. "Patched through."

Jack angled the nose of the airship down and hovered over a small maize field, thrusters causing ripples through the stalks like water. "This is Captain Jack McGraw of the airship *Daedalus*. We represent the Allied Enterprise Group for International Security, and mean you no harm. Please come out and speak with us."

The farm's outbuildings sat in a semicircle at the northern border of the cornfield, extending from the great house, which bore an English colonial design in stark contrast to the timber, mud and thatch dwellings of the Kikuyu. Bloodied corpses of native farm workers lay silent, strewn haphazardly from the fields to the great house stoop. The house itself would have been considered a quaint cottage back in England, yet it dwarfed all other construction on the local acreage.

As the crew watched from the bridge viewport, the house took on a golden-orange hue, and black smoke began to waft from seams in the roof. Flames surged outward and windows shattered, and a single figure appeared in the front doorway. He was a huge man, shirtless and dark, with some kind of metal vambraces and homespun leggings. His face was painted in the approximation of a white, grinning skull, and he clutched a pair of blades, sub--Saharan variants on the Egyptian *khopesh,* terminating in hooked claws at their tips.

As the enormous skull-painted man stepped nonchalantly down the wooden steps of the great house, the ever-growing flames framed him in the colors of sunset, though it was not even noon. Gradually, several others, perhaps a dozen in all, men and women from twenty to sixty years of age, began to appear from behind the outbuildings and the burning great house. Another four crept from the cornfield. They carried rakes and scythes. Some had Enfield rifles.

"Captain," Cipher said softly and ominously. "Permission to go ashore."

Jack blinked. "What? Are you cr—?"

"We need to find out what's going on here," she answered. "And to my knowledge, I'm the only one on this ship who speaks Swahili."

Doc sighed and leaned over to Jack. "She's right. And besides, if these locals are fighting the British, it might be good to lead with a face that doesn't look like another white invader."

Jack scowled, but he couldn't argue with their logic. "Fine," he acquiesced. "But I want Deadeye on your flank with his Winchester. And if you get into any trouble out there, you get back on the ship in a hurry, got it?"

"Yes, Captain," Cipher nodded, swiveling in her seat and releasing her safety harness.

As she disappeared through the hatch into the main saloon, Jack's face screwed into a tight mask of paternal stress and military readiness.

Doc noticed the sudden, subtle tension and caressed his shoulder. "Easy, Jack," she said as she gently kneaded his trapezius, eliciting a groan of approval. "She'll be alright."

- CHAPTER 2 -

Cipher opened the side door on the gondola and dropped to the dusty ground, followed by Deadeye. Though the Cherokee had his repeating rifle at the ready, he knew they'd be immediately outgunned if a fight broke out.

Cipher looked official enough in her navy blue paramilitary uniform trousers and black officer's boots. Though her gray cotton field shirt was unbuttoned to the collarbone and the sleeves rolled above the elbow, her red beret with its AEGIS winged shield patch lent an air of authority. She kept her sidearm holstered and her hands open.

Deadeye wore his usual khaki field trousers and *puttees*, with a sweat-stained white t-shirt and no head cover. He scanned the front of the farmhouse, noting which natives were armed with rifles, and which would have to cover ground to get to the *Daedalus*.

The large man with the painted skull face strode slowly and powerfully to meet Cipher, who, despite her instincts, stepped forward in greeting.

"*Salamu,*" she said in Swahili. "*Jina langu ni* Cipher."

The giant man stared at her a moment, while Deadeye's thumb played over the hammer of the Winchester. Finally, the painted skull squinted, and the man's head thrust forward.

"*Mimi ni Bwana Kifo,*" he said, adding curiously, and in flawless English, "but you don't look Kikuyu."

Cipher was taken aback momentarily. Did the giant man say his name was *Mister Death*? Her translation couldn't be that far off. "No, I am not Kikuyu," she stammered. "I am Punjabi."

"India," the man discerned. "And your friend?" he said, nodding at Deadeye.

"Cherokee," Cipher answered.

"America," said the man.

"Yes," Cipher smiled. "You are well-educated."

"Do not patronize me," the man straightened and turned his left side to face her. "Are you here to help the British, or to help us?"

"Is that who you are fighting? The British?"

"The magistrate in Voi is Major Edwards. It is he whose blood my blades thirst for." The skull-faced man cast a glance at Deadeye, who gripped the walnut stock of the carbine a bit more tightly.

Cipher's brow furrowed. "Bwana Kifo," she said, "what has happened here?"

The man clenched his jaw, hesitant to speak for a time. Finally: "The white settler who runs this farm claimed a native worker assaulted his wife. Major Edwards had the worker arrested and taken to the garrison in Voi, where he was beaten and shot, without trial. When the farm workers protested outside the garrison, they too were shot. This ill treatment of the workers angered the local Kikuyu chieftains, who began to raid the farms of the white settlers late last night. In reprisal, the Major called out the whole garrison to punish the villages."

Cipher looked beyond the massive warrior and scanned the faces of the natives behind him. They looked haggard, yet determined. "Does the Governor know of this conflict?"

Bwana Kifo lowered his frustrated gaze to meet her brown eyes. "I do not know," he sighed. "But if he does, more soldiers will not be far behind."

Cipher pressed her palms together. "If we intercede with the Governor on behalf of the Kikuyu, will you stand down?"

Suddenly a runner in short pants and sandals appeared by the dwelling nearest the burning farmhouse. His skinny torso heaved with breath, showing a lattice of ribs with each inhalation. "*Bwana Kifo! Askari kuja!*"

"Soldiers!" the giant man turned. All faces became set with a dire intent.

"Please," Cipher interjected. "We can help, if you just—"

Bwana Kifo spun back to her, his skull face just inches from her own. "If you want to help these people, follow me. Otherwise, leave in peace."

Then he was gone, moving beyond the farmhouse to the trail head and into the scrub at supernatural speed. The natives and farm workers followed, leaving Cipher and Deadeye staring after them, slack-jawed.

☙

The *Daedalus* came in low over the scrub of the eastern savanna. The village was already afire, swarming with natives and British soldiers in khaki short fatigues and a mix of pith helmets and turbans. Jack had Asim take the stick, while he, Deadeye, and Cipher went to the open gondola door. Doc began to protest that the ship's medic should be present, but Jack persuaded her to wait until they had the situation on the ground under control.

Asim brought the ship down low in a soft turn, the linked forward guns erupting in a chatter of hot lead to cover the trio's departure. Then it rose into the air again, taking up a support position in the sky above the village.

Jack's feet hit the hard, sun-baked dirt and he sprang from a squat, coming up with both Colts drawn. Cipher landed and whirled around to cover their six, Webley service revolver at the ready. Deadeye levered the Winchester in midair, taking aim as he stuck his own landing.

Before the dust from the airship's thrusters could clear, a group of half a dozen soldiers formed up in a firing line, raising their Enfield rifles squarely at the trio who had dropped from the sky just moments before.

Cipher turned and noticed their turbans, and her heart sank. They were Indian—Sikh, specifically—being used as the personal murder squad of a British officer on a rampage. Deadeye took aim and Jack stepped forward to pull some kind of rank, although he hadn't been a military officer since the Great War. Still, his commission had been with the British Army, so it was worth a shot.

But before he could utter the phrase, "Stand down, men!" Cipher stepped in front of him, waving her hands frantically and shouting at the soldiers in Punjabi.

"Khaṛhē rahō! Asīṁ dōsata hāṁ!"

The soldiers paused, glancing between Cipher and each other. Then the corporal shrugged and ran off toward the hut of the village chieftain, the rest of the soldiers following.

As they crossed in front of the trail head, a huge form leaped into the village, blades slicing through air and flesh. Within moments, the soldiers were blasted apart as if by an explosive weapon—this weapon being Bwana Kifo and his dual *khopesh*. Before Jack could even warn him to stop, the huge man had bowled through the unit of British soldiers, and moved on to the force already gathered around the chieftain's dwelling.

"What's his name? Kifo?" Jack hollered at Cipher as they ran after the giant, painted man.

Cipher nodded. "Bwana Kifo. Mister Death."

Delightful, Jack thought as they tried to make up the distance. *But then, my call sign is 'Captain Stratosphere', so what do I know?*

They arrived in front of the tribal dwelling and had only scant moments to take in the scene: A young Kikuyu woman, in her early twenties at most, knelt in the doorway, clutching the body of an older native man in her lap. Like most of the local Kikuyu, she wore functional western clothing: a dun-colored cotton safari shirt and trousers, with leather work boots. Her black hair was tightly braided and pulled back under a stained, gray bandanna. The man she held looked to be in his fifties, hair and beard frosted with a touch of white. He'd also been shot in the chest, and had been dead for at least several minutes.

The line of British soldiers faced the door to the dwelling at a distance of perhaps twenty paces, rifles raised and ready to shoot. Jack paused momentarily, wondering why a group of soldiers would be preparing to shoot an unarmed woman who was clearly grieving the loss of someone close to her. Suddenly, from the corner of his eye, he noticed another soldier fire at a herd of penned goats across the square. There was an angry shriek, and a Kikuyu woman rushed out of her dwelling to confront the soldier. The soldier produced a service revolver from his belt and, without so much as a word, shot her in the head.

Jack waved his arms, trying to get the attention of the semicircle of British Indian soldiers. "Wait! Stop!" he warned.

A shadow fell across the woman in the hut's doorway, and Bwana Kifo landed as if having fallen from orbit. His massive chest rose and fell, blood leaking from wounds both severe and superficial. His swords were streaked red, glistening in the noonday sunlight. The painted skull on his dark features looked as though it was prepared to escort someone—or many someones—straight to hell.

The rifles fired, a great eruption of sulfur smoke and hot lead.

Bwana Kifo fell.

Deadeye fired into the squad, knocking rifles from stunned hands.

Jack and Cipher moved in, creating a second wall between the soldiers and the distraught young woman in the hut.

"Drop 'em!" Jack ordered, brandishing the Colts. "Drop 'em NOW!"

One soldier stepped forward in a physical challenge, but Jack was prepared for resistance. Moving forward, he flipped the pistol in his left hand high into the air. As the soldier instinctively glanced upward, Jack grabbed the man's rifle with his left hand and landed a solid pistol whip with his right, dropping him where he stood. In a single motion, his left hand dispensed of the Enfield rifle and caught the falling Colt.

Both pistols were back in the faces of the soldiers. "I have had enough of you blokes today," he bellowed through clenched teeth. "Don't make me tell you again."

Cipher moved behind Jack to check on the large man the soldiers had cut down just moments before, and Deadeye stepped to Jack's right, keeping a watchful gaze on the proceedings.

Of the eight soldiers facing Jack, only two still held weapons, which were quickly dropped.

"Now," Jack said, visibly angry, "I don't know what your orders were from Major Edwards, but if it was a cleansing of the local villages, then all of you—and Major Edwards—are in a lot of trouble."

A corporal, in khaki field dress and matching turban, opened his mouth to protest. Jack was on him inside of a second, the nickel-finish of a Colt pistol gleaming as it pressed into the soldier's forehead.

"Not a word, soldier," said Jack, shaking his head. "Not one word."

Deadeye shifted uncomfortably. He didn't think for a moment that his captain would actually shoot an unarmed foe in the head, but even the bluff made him uneasy.

Jack pulled the pistol from the man's head and backed a few paces away. "I want you to turn around and go back to the garrison right now. Leave your rifles and sidearms here and go. Any more British troops we see in this—or any—village today will be targets. The AEGIS airship *Daedalus* is engaged in the defense of the local Kikuyu people."

As the soldiers slowly turned and wandered away into the low scrub, Jack shouted after them. "And tell Major Edwards we're going to pay him a visit, with the weight of the Crown and the Foreign Office behind us."

The soldiers disappeared, and Jack and Deadeye were left standing in the village square, the smoke from rifles and burning homes swirling around them. Deadeye took up a watch position near the door of the chieftain's home, and Jack went to help Cipher with the body of Bwana Kifo.

"He's dead," Cipher pronounced as Jack knelt at her side.

Sure enough, the freedom fighter's broad chest had been sundered by a half dozen rifle slugs. If one had pieced his heart, it would have killed him instantly. Jack holstered his pistols and bent to grip Bwana Kifo under his arms. With Cipher hefting his legs, they were able to move him out of the way, laying him gently in the village square.

Deadeye peered around through the door. The young woman returned his gaze, tears now drying on her cheeks. "I'm Charlie. What's your name?" the sharpshooter asked.

"Dhakiya," she answered.

Jack and Cipher returned to the hut, both crouching by the woman and her dead relation.

"*Sisi ni marafiki*," Cipher assured.

Jack nodded. "We're friends."

"I speak English," said the woman.

Jack glanced down at the dead body sprawled across her lap, head cradled gently in her hands. "I'm very sorry," he said earnestly.

"My father," she said. "He was Chief."

Deadeye made a visual sweep of the village to see that, aside from some livestock left un-slaughtered, they were the only souls left in the area. "We oughta think about leaving soon, Cap."

Jack suddenly did a double-take. "Did you say your name was Dhakiya?"

The woman nodded. "Dhakiya Kitur. I was a mechanic at the British airfield at Mombasa. But now..."

"Now you're the chief engineer on the airship *Daedalus*," Jack said.

Her eyes widened and she shook cobwebs of grief and trauma from her head. "Thank you for what you did with those soldiers."

"This attack on your people will not go unaddressed," Cipher promised sternly.

"Can you travel?" asked Jack.

Dhakiya nodded, wiping away the stale tears from her face. "When the dead have been buried."

By instinct, Deadeye scanned the village square once again, blinking as he compared this time with his recollection of the last. "Speaking of which," the marksman muttered, "we seem to be one corpse short."

Jack and Cipher both turned to look, coming to the same realization at the same time. The spot where they'd dragged the giant, painted African was now suspiciously minus the body they'd left there. Bwana Kifo was gone.

- CHAPTER 3 -

Using the pneumatic pitons furnished by AEGIS, the *Daedalus* was tied down for a couple hours as her crew dug graves and buried bodies in the afternoon heat. When the hard labor was finished, they let the livestock go and boarded the airship, exhausted and sweating, to head to Mombasa.

Otherwise based in Nairobi, the British governor of Kenya happened to be in town for the week, touring military and shipping facilities, and Jack and Doc made a plan to intercept him at dinner.

By the time the *Daedalus* and *Percival* rendezvoused at RAF Mombasa, the sun was dipping below the horizon. The temperature remained sultry, and the flying insects came out in force. The *Daedalus* crew, still sore from having buried more than thirty people in the heat of the day, were able to shower off and change into presentable clothes. Although word of the crew's disruption of an official Army operation had reached the airfield prior to their arrival, too many people knew of the heroic exploits of Captain "Stratosphere" Jack McGraw and Commander Edward "Duke" Willis to believe the unhinged reports coming from the garrison in Voi. Major Edwards' orders were that the crew of the *Daedalus* were to be arrested on sight, but Duke had already radioed back to Sir Harold Marston in Cairo, who had placed a long-distance telephone call to The Right Honorable Edward Grigg, Governor of Kenya, to intercede on behalf of the AEGIS field agents.

Representatives of the airship crews converged on the dining lounge at the Metropole Hotel. Doc sat in the bar alongside Aussie pilot Sheila Barrett of the *Percival*, while Jack, Cipher, Dhakiya, and Duke went to sit at Governor Grigg's table and plead their case.

Grigg took great pride in his cosmopolitan background and years of service to the Crown. Born in British India, he'd served with decorated distinction in France during the Great War, ending up a lieutenant-colonel. After the war, he'd been Military Secretary to the Prince of Wales and a Liberal MP in the House of

Commons before accepting the post of colonial governor. Under his administration, Kenya was growing. Already improvements to education and infrastructure could be seen, and yet, like most colonial administrators, he was not ready to enfranchise the indigenous people with the running of their own affairs. Those old attitudes trickled down through the ranks, where petty tyrants like Major Edwards felt execution without trial was an acceptable practice. He certainly wasn't the first, nor unfortunately would he be the last.

Grigg chose his words carefully as he washed a bite of rare steak down with a glass of imported French Bordeaux. "I can rightly say that I don't agree with the steps the major took in response to the uprising, but under law, he has the authority."

"With all due respect, sir," Cipher countered, "the uprising did not originate out of thin air."

Duke nodded in agreement. "Too true. What of the man who was denied due process? We cannot pick and choose when to invoke rule of law and when to conveniently look away. If the Empire is to function properly, the rule of law must apply equally to rich and poor alike, the laborer and the lord."

Grigg was struck by Duke's passion on the topic. "I see your point, Commander. But what action do you expect me to take?"

"What action would you take against a rogue officer guilty of a war crime?" Cipher posited, and Grigg's eyes grew wide at the suggestion.

Duke followed her comment with the answer: "Arrest and court martial."

"It's the least you can do," Cipher suggested. "Lawlessness and murder don't look good under any administration, not to mention yours."

The governor angrily picked through a small pile of over-boiled greens, staring at his fork. "Major Edwards is well-connected," he said. "At best, he'll be stripped of his commission and sent back to England in disgrace. At worst, he could employ his own resources to seek revenge, and that is not a result I would enjoy."

Jack finally spoke. "Which serves the greater good?" he asked. It sounded a bit trite, a bit jingoistic, but it was fundamentally the right question to ask. It seemed to calm the governor's somewhat heated frame of mind.

There was a long pause as Grigg contemplated his next move, his next words. "Alright," he said finally, clearing his throat as he went. "I owe Sir Harold a favor or three, and we'll call two of them your amnesty and Edwards' court martial."

"Thank you, sir," Duke nodded.

Jack leaned forward, his face underlit by a candle in the middle of the table. "If I may, Governor..."

Grigg nodded, leaning back in his chair, truly curious at what the famous fighter ace had to say.

Jack met the governor's gaze and clenched his hands into fists that he held absolutely still on the table. "If you do this, do it all the way. Go in strong and keep Edwards on the defensive. Don't give him any inkling that his revenge is a concern. Let him know—let him see—that you hold *all* the cards. AEGIS will back you up."

Governor Grigg stared at his wine glass and nodded solemnly. So there it was. The governor issued an official pardon to the AEGIS operatives involved in the Voi Tribal Uprising. Major Edwards would find himself up on charges by the following morning, and standing court martial once back in Nairobi. The local Kikuyu would receive an official apology and some money to help rebuild their villages and lives. The Indian soldiers involved in the massacre would be separated, absorbed into other units and re-deployed elsewhere.

Even as the parties at the table in the Metropole came to agreement, Jack couldn't help but think that this was only the beginning of strife and upheaval in East Africa. The sooner the airships could be underway, the better for all of them.

That night in Mombasa would be the last one on the ground for some time.

☙

Dhakiya Kitur had never flown before. She was a naturally gifted mechanic and knew internal combustion engines and electrical systems inside and out, making her a valued member of the ground crew at RAF Mombasa, but she'd never actually gone up in a plane, or even an observation balloon. In the shock of losing her father in the massacre, she'd all but blocked out the short flight from her home village to the airfield at Mombasa. Now Doc was giving her an official tour of the craft which would become her home.

They stood on the tarmac in the wan light of the moon and a few exterior lanterns, gazing over the elegant, almost shark-like lozenge tied to the deck cleats. Though her envelope was a semi-reflective silver, it shone a strange blue-orange in the mixed evening light. The

Percival's tail section was visible past the nose of the *Daedalus*, several meters distant.

"You're formally trained in engineering and mechanics?" Doc asked the young girl.

"Because my father was chief, I went to a British school in Nairobi. They saw my aptitude and sent me to university in Cairo."

Doc was impressed. "That's outstanding," she marveled.

Dhakiya squinted at the registration number on the aft flank of the *Daedalus* envelope. "L-R-3?"

"LR stands for Light Reconnaissance, and this is the third *Daedalus*-class vessel," Doc explained. "The first was a prototype built by Vincenzo DiMarco, who also developed the electric dynamos that generate our power. The second one I had the pleasure of serving aboard for two years. We took her all over, through the Caribbean, the Amazon, into the Himalayas. The new version went into production in March of this year. She's already been across the Atlantic, through Europe, to Greece, Egypt, and down the Nile."

"She's beautiful," Dhakiya said softly, unsure that this moment, like the earlier events of the day, was real. Her nose wrinkled and she wiped away a tear before it could fall.

Doc noticed her awkward discomfort. "Dhakiya," she said, touching the young mechanic softly on the shoulder, "you don't have to do this. You can stay here in Mombasa. We don't want to take you away from any family or—"

"My family is dead," Dhakiya stated firmly. "The only reason to stay would be to punish Major Edwards."

"But it sounds as if that's been taken care of."

"Only by white law," Dhakiya spat. "And white law is not justice."

Doc nodded. She wanted to believe the British Empire and other world powers had the best interest of their subjects at heart, but she'd seen otherwise and knew better. "I know," she said. "And I would never diminish the struggle of the Kikuyu people. But if you come with us, I guarantee you will be of use to a greater good." Doc met Dhakiya's brown eyes and her tone became earnest. "There's a force at work—a limitless evil—which is bent on destroying all of civilization, enslaving all people, casting our world into endless darkness. That is what we fight. That is our battle."

"That is the evil Bwana Kifo has spoken of," Dhakiya replied.

"Yes, your 'Mister Death'." Doc's eyes narrowed. "I've been meaning to ask you how you know him, and how he was able to disappear after being shot multiple times at close range."

It was now Dhakiya's turn to lecture. "Bwana Kifo is one of the *Walezi*," she said. "They are guardians of all Africa. He is not Kikuyu and does not come from here. *Odinani* priests made him what he is."

Doc pursed her lips, curious. "And what exactly is he?"

"He is the living embodiment of *Ogu na Ofo*."

"I'm not familiar with that term."

"It is the concept of retributive justice," Dhakiya said.

"I see," said Doc. The skeptic in her had questions, but the experienced occultist in her had witnessed Haitian *zombis,* demonic summonings and dark magic at work. Heck, she even had a severed demon arm packed away in a secret warehouse in New Jersey. "So how do you think Bwana Kifo would counsel you?"

The young woman furrowed her brow in thought. In most cases, the death of the chieftain would result in the transfer of power to the eldest child, or the chieftain's sibling if his offspring were children. But her line of the Kikuyu people had been all but exterminated. Any individuals would be absorbed by the other villages and chieftains. She could claim power, but power over what? Some half-burned huts and empty goat pens? No, there was only one choice to be made here.

"Like Bwana Kifo, I have seen evil at work in the world. I am no stranger to its hunger for the lives of innocents." Dhakiya gave Doc a square look and the smallest hint of a smile. "I will go with you. I will fight."

☙

Major Edwards awoke at dawn to the sound of British Military Police at his door. The next twenty minutes were all bluster and indignation and unending complaint, as Edwards furiously paced his quarters, throwing on his uniform. When one of the officers relieved him of his service revolver, leaving him only with a swagger stick, Edwards swore a blue streak until the officer threatened, "The Major will kindly be silent, or the Major will be gagged."

Governor Grigg was waiting for him outside the garrison with a military transport truck and a new unit of riflemen. When Edwards saw a fresh captain at the head of the rank, he frowned and went straight at Grigg.

"I say, what the devil—"

"You're relieved of your post, Major Edwards," Grigg offered perfunctorily. "And potentially your commission, depending upon the results of your court martial."

"Court martial?" Edwards sputtered. "Now see here—!"

Taking Jack's advice from the prior evening to heart, Grigg was aggressive and all business. "You're a bloody disgrace, Major. Your charge was to administer the King's law in this township, not murder the native workers for some perceived slight without due process of said law." Grigg strode to him and peered through eyes illuminated by the garrison gaslight. "Not under my administration. You will be held to account, sir."

He nodded to the police officers and they escorted the major to the rear of the truck. The captain approached and saluted, and Grigg returned the gesture.

"Captain Meredith," he said, "you are now in command of this garrison, and must clean up Major Edwards' mess. I trust you can find the golden mean between keeping discipline and abusing your authority."

A sharp-featured Welshman with dark hair and gleaming blue eyes, Meredith snapped his heels together at attention. "Indeed, sir! You can trust in me, sir!"

Grigg nodded at him. "Very good, Captain. Carry on."

"Very good, sir!" Meredith saluted once more, then turned to wave his troops into the garrison.

The Military Police officers finished securing Edwards in the back of the transport truck. Governor Grigg strode to the driver's door, speaking through the unrolled window.

"Take him to the garrison in Nairobi. I'll be along by train this afternoon."

The driver saluted, watching as the Governor strode away toward his parked motorcar, flanked by his secretary and a native Kenyan bodyguard. He angled the large side view mirror, catching sight of two airships rising into the sky from RAF Mombasa, miles away. Had anyone been standing beside the truck at that moment, they would have noticed the black outline of a four-pointed star tattooed inside his wrist.

As the sun rose and life in the British Empire struggled back to a semblance of normalcy, the transport truck rattled to a start, and rolled away onto the road to Nairobi.

ℭℜ

"That's affirmative," Cipher spoke into her collar microphone. "Course heading northeast to Bombay. Will rendezvous Alexandra Dock. *Daedalus* over and out."

"*Percival* over and out," came the reply over the comm speakers.

Jack eased the stick back and throttled forward, the engines' electric whine rising in pitch. He hit the *TALK* button on the pilot's console, his smooth baritone echoing throughout the ship: to the main saloon, where Asim sat drinking coffee; to the engine room, where a wide-eyed Dhakiya pored over technical manuals; to the top turret, where Deadeye dozed quietly, snuggled into his harness. "Captain to crew. We're a little over 2700 miles to Bombay. That's about 34 hours at cruising speed, which we dare not push as each ship is minus one dynamo. With a good tailwind, we might shave some time off. Other than that, you all have your stations and know your duties. Standard four-hour watches. Carry on."

Doc double-checked their course on her navigational chart and glanced at her watch to note the time. All was in order, and there wasn't any extreme weather activity in the immediate vicinity. The sun was just coming up over the Indian Ocean, an orange and gold fireworks display among the pink morning clouds. "It's too bad we're not venturing any further north once we hit Bombay," she remarked. "It'd be nice to see Padger again." She recalled the aged, hard-drinking RAF pilot they'd met in the Himalayas the previous year. It was his Bristol "Biff" she and Jack had "borrowed", crashing it in a lost thermal valley where previously undiscovered animal species roamed, and plants with potentially powerful medicinal uses grew wild. Padger had been compensated with a brand new Boeing Model 40-A, so couldn't bring himself to hold a grudge. Besides, the dirty old man clearly had a thing for Doc. Most men did, eventually. Either that, or they ran screaming into the night. There was usually very little middle-ground.

"True enough," Jack agreed. "It'd be good to see how he's doing with his new plane and courier business."

"Because you crashed the old one," Doc smiled.

Jack turned in the pilot's chair and pointed at his headset, shaking his head and miming a bad transmission.

"Oh stop," scolded Doc. "I know we can't stray from our course. The Silver Star has Rivets captive, and we need to rescue him."

"Darn right," Jack scowled. He glanced over his shoulder at Cipher. "Lieutenant Singh, I want your ear to the ground, so to speak, and on alert for any radio-detector contact matching the *Osiris* or *Luftpanzer II*."

"Aye, Captain," came her reply.

"And now, let's settle in," Jack muttered, bringing the throttle to cruising speed.

As the sun rose in the eastern sky, Jack squinted and plucked the pack of Black Jack gum from his chest pocket, fishing the last stick from the waxed paper wrapper.

Drat. He hadn't prepared for their spring mission in Scotland to become a trek into Africa in the high summer. Perhaps they would have some chewing gum available in Bombay. Or Bangkok, their next stop. Although he preferred the pungent black licorice flavor of Black Jack, really any variety would suffice. It equalized the air pressure in his ears, and gave him an alternative to the cigarillos he'd smoked briefly during the war. Training in hydrogen-filled airships had weaned him from that particular flammable habit, but Jack McGraw was a man of ritual, and he'd replaced that one with Black Jack.

He would savor this last stick as he watched the sunlight glimmer on the surface of the Indian Ocean half a mile below them.

- CHAPTER 4 -

Bombay was alive and surging with crowds of people. The late-morning heat and high humidity made the air thick and laborious to breathe. With the *Daedalus* and *Percival* tied down at Alexandra Dock in the southeastern part of the island, a foraging party emerged to check in with the customs house, and procure supplies from the local mercantile area. Four AEGIS field agents emerged from the airships at the dock, clad in navy blue uniform trousers, black boots, light gray cotton shirts unbuttoned to the chest, their sleeves rolled up to the elbows. One wore an officer's cap, one a red beret. The other two wore light canvas bush hats and dark glasses. The four each carried a holstered sidearm on a wide, cotton web belt.

Sir Arthur Crawford Market buzzed with the activity of buying and selling, the colorful crafts and wares topped only by the scents of ginger, cardamom, cinnamon, turmeric, and various chilis and curry spices. Stalls selling caged songbirds, incense or "authentic" ancient artifacts competed with the sidewalk cobra charmers and pierced *fakirs* for attention and the odd *rupee*. Trolley cars crawled past the ranks of outdoor carts to the main entrance of the grand market itself, which boasted even higher-quality wares in an indoor shopping environment away from the merciless sun outside.

Duke and Cipher formed one team, tasked with procuring food, tea, and any information they could drum up regarding the two Silver Star airships they were chasing. Jack and Doc formed the other team, looking for maps or charts of the greater Oceania region. Both teams would be on the lookout for some things Dhakiya had scrawled in a list:

Copper wire, 13.5 meter spool

Lead solder

KS steel or ferrite magnets, 20

Platinum cathodes, 2

"The heck is a platinum cathode?" Jack mused, scratching his head under the floppy brim of the bush hat.

Doc smiled. She loved seeing Jack out of his element as much as in it. "Probably has to do with making hydrogen on the fly," she said. "I only know because Rivets tried to show me the process back in New Jersey. These might be replacements for the current parts."

"Whatever they're for," Jack muttered, "We're not likely to find them in a public market in Bombay."

"True," Doc agreed.

Jack was beginning to think Cipher, being Punjabi with a command of the local dialects, would have far better luck obtaining the items on the list than he. But that didn't mean he wouldn't try. And if they somehow duplicated efforts, Dhakiya would have spare parts to work with.

The market was nestled between the rail lines at Victoria Terminus and Esplanade Cross Road. Jack and Doc headed north, toward the array of stalls and produce carts, the enormous sprawl of Native Town rising beyond the Esplanade.

They worked their way through a crowd watching a *fakir* balancing a sword on his head while striking various yoga poses. Jack felt a hand test at his back pocket and swipe up the left side of his ribcage. By instinct, he grabbed the mystery hand and pressed a nerve cluster in the wrist, releasing the paralyzed limb back into the mass of people. One fewer able pickpocket in the market. Not a bad thing at all. He smiled to himself, knowing that his identification, travel papers, and money were tucked away somewhere only he or his doctor could access without a fight.

"What was that?" Doc asked. "You okay?"

Jack nodded. "Fine. Just hunky dory."

"Cipher told me about a map shop across the Esplanade," said Doc. "Let's go check it out."

"Don't let me forget," Jack added, "I'm out of gum."

The two continued through the crowds, watchful eyes peering through dark, round lenses. They both knew Bombay by reputation. It was a mercantile city of great wealth concentrated at the top, mostly among the British administrators, and great poverty at the bottom. Like most metropolises throughout the world, it was inhabited by a majority of decent, hard-working people, squeezed from all sides by those with power, money, or an agenda. Pirates from both sides of the Arabian Sea traded their ill-gotten wares in the numerous markets, of both the sanctioned and black variety. Though considered extinct by authorities of the British Raj, the Thuggee cult had resurfaced in recent years and was active in the area, preying upon travelers heading to the interior. Elements of the Black Brotherhood, devotees of an ancient, eldritch pantheon, were gaining a foothold in the poorer sections of the city, as well. Of course, where there were poor, disaffected people, there was the *Astrum Argentum*—the Silver Star—with their promises of money and power and respect. These promises came with two small caveats: 1) Said money, power, and respect might never arrive; at least not all of them, and not all at once. 2) The cost was your soul, up front. No refunds.

Doc scanned ahead for anything unusual. The locals dressed in colorful, loose-fitting *shalwar* suits, silk *saris* and *phulkari*, all loose enough to hide a weapon—perhaps even a blowgun for administering a lethal poison. That very fate had befallen her late husband, Colonel Dirk Starr, in Venezuela five years ago. She wasn't about to let history repeat if she could help it.

Just as she was finishing the thought and they cleared the crowd, "Doc! Look out!" erupted from her left and something big pushed her into an open cobblestone square. She staggered forward and spun to see Jack reaching across his body for the pistol at his left hip. A Marathi man in a gold and white *shalwar* suit and saffron turban had squared off with him, hand outstretched as if he'd just thrown something. Somewhere behind them, a woman screamed and fell to the ground. The gleaming steel handle of a throwing blade protruded from her chest.

Doc squinted. The inside of the man's wrist was tattooed with a four-pointed star. It was the same concave diamond shape she'd seen on planes, airships, and the hat and collar insignia of countless Silver Star agents, from the Amazon to Africa. She also knew whenever they encountered it, it meant they were on the right track. She turned back toward the crowd to see about helping the woman hit by the would-be assassin's blade.

As Jack reached down across to his left, unsnapping the canvas holster and skinning the nickel-plated .45 from within, the assassin let fly a second blade. It impacted the side of the pistol, knocking it away toward a group of young street urchins. Jack instinctively reached across to his right, where he usually carried the first pistol's twin, but they'd only brought a single weapon apiece. "Drat," he muttered, watching the assassin closely. If he remained at this range, he would end up a human knife-rack for sure. The best thing to do would be to close the distance and engage the assailant in some good old fashioned fisticuffs.

Doc knelt at the side of the fallen woman. She was perhaps forty, in a blue *sari* and matching pantaloons. The blade had impacted about four inches to the right of her left shoulder, in the breastbone above the heart. Doc removed her own canvas hat and rolled it up as a makeshift pillow. She was just sliding it under the victim's head when the woman sputtered and coughed an unexpected amount of blood onto herself. Her eyes rolled back in their sockets, and her breath stopped cold with a shudder. Doc's eyes snapped wide and she ripped the dark glasses from her face.

Jack leaped forward, right arm cocked back to punch. Behind him, he heard, "Jack! Be careful! The blades are poisoned!"

His punch landed, the assassin stumbling backward into the square. As the man staggered, another throwing blade left his hand. Jack instinctively put his left arm up to block, knocking the blade away to the ground. He strode forward, unwilling to give the assailant a moment's respite. Another right cross hit home, shattering the assassin's jaw. A left jab to the torso bent the man in half, and a powerful right uppercut finished the job. The assassin splayed out in the open square, and Jack stooped to retrieve his Colt from the curious hands of an eight-year-old beggar. He flipped the kid a coin and stood upright, scanning the crowd for Doc, finding her just as a gunman opened fire with a Browning Assault Rifle from a second story window across the Esplanade.

"Jeez!" Jack shouted, as they ducked away behind a cart selling locally-grown jackfruit and mangoes. "Really?" Behind them in the square, the knife-thrower's body began to sizzle and smoke like burning butter in a skillet.

"Someone knew we were here," said Doc, unholstering her .38. "And they don't want us to leave."

"No kidding!" Jack scanned the produce stalls to the east of the open square. They were laid out in three rows before the rail line formed a barrier to further sprawl. To the west lay Market Road, full of motor and horse-buggy traffic. "No good options," he said. "We have to work toward him, try to get under his firing arc."

Doc looked around at the screaming throngs of people dodging this way and that, flinging themselves prone on the ground, or running for the cover of the market building. He was right. East or west meant too many civilians in peril. "I'm with you, handsome," she said, spinning the chamber on her revolver. "Let's go."

Jack stood, and suddenly there were three pistols in three hands, and Doc had an identical twin sister. His vision began to pulse and vibrate in time to his heartbeat, a blurry black curtain drawing in from the outside.

Doc turned to see his left arm stained crimson, oozing blood from the open wound.

"Doc?" he wheezed, confused at why his ears suddenly felt like they'd been packed with cotton. "I feel a little..."

Doc swept in, cushioning his fall as best she could, but unable to keep Jack's large frame from crashing through the mango cart, spilling fruit everywhere. She cradled his head and looked around desperately for help.

"No, Jack... Oh no."

- CHAPTER 5 -

Duke pushed past a fig vendor and an old man with a trained monkey on a leash. He was used to the human tidal currents of open markets throughout the Empire, having served in the Royal Army in China, India, and Northern Africa. Bombay was similar in scale and population to other major centers of commerce he'd visited. He actually found the proximity to so many fellow humans comforting.

Cipher caught up with him, holding open a greasy paper bag. "*Samosas?*" she offered. "Freshly made."

Duke ambled to the side of the street and reached into the bag, producing a fried pastry stuffed with potatoes and spices. "Thank you, Lieutenant," he said in his posh English accent—pronouncing it *'leftenant'*. "I do love a good *samosa*." As he savored the exotic spices and textures of the pastry, Duke let down his guard. "You did rather good work back there in Kenya."

Cipher took her time absorbing the compliment. She looked up to Duke as a mentor, an officer, and an AEGIS field agent, but she'd seen the dark underbelly of the Empire of which they were both a product. "I did what needed to be done, Commander," she explained. "It wasn't easy seeing my countrymen used to murder innocents."

"Indeed not," Duke agreed solemnly. "Indeed not. But the villain responsible will by now be facing the consequences."

Cipher tried to look convinced, but failed.

The staccato drumbeat of automatic gunfire suddenly erupted from the other end of the market, and Cipher immediately dropped the bag, skinning her Webley service revolver from its canvas holster.

Duke moved forward, hand on his own holster, but not drawn. "This way," he instructed.

Together they shoved their way upstream against the counter-current of shoppers and merchants trying to escape the gunfire. Duke peered into the distance, noting a brief muzzle flash erupting from a second story window in a building on the far side of the Esplanade

Cross Road. He estimated the gunman's position and flagged Cipher. "See if you can locate Doc and the Captain," he instructed, gesturing to their left. "They should be somewhere in that direction—"

"Where the gunfire is aimed." Cipher swallowed dryly, despite the humidity. "Where are you going?"

"We passed a telegraph office at the Terminus," Duke said sternly. "I'm getting some help."

Then Duke was gone, and Cipher found herself staring down a gauntlet of food carts and produce stalls which offered scarce protection against a machine gun with a superior vantage point.

Hunched over and scurrying from cart to cart, Cipher made her way delicately through the maze of wooden stalls, sending fallen produce skittering in front of her as she moved toward the open square. Her motion caught the attention of the gunman, and suddenly her world was awash in exploding mangoes and papayas, cabbages and tomatoes. Splinters of wood whipped past her face. A spinning iron nail split her right cheek. She dove to the cobbled street and threw her arms across her face until the barrage of gunfire let up.

When the gun fell silent, Cipher scrambled into a sitting position behind the wooden frame of a bakery stand that had been selling garlic *naan*. Flats of oven-cooked bread were strewn around a ten-meter radius, and the fabric sunshade hung in shreds from the arm of the awning. She reached up and felt her face slick with blood. Peering around the side of the stall, she saw seven turbaned agents approaching the open square from across the Esplanade. Each was dressed in robes of black and crimson, and carried an MP-18 submachine gun—the favored weapon of Silver Star soldiers everywhere.

She could see the produce cart some thirty meters distant, a crude obstacle between the approaching soldiers and Doc, who had flung herself across the unconscious form of Jack McGraw. Cipher's breath caught in her throat. *Was the captain dead?*

If she made a run for Doc, the gunmen would certainly see her. On the upside, it might draw their fire enough for Doc and the captain to make an escape. Although, thinking it through, Doc hadn't remained in her current location merely because she'd been pinned down by the machine gun firing from the window across the street; she was still there because she couldn't physically move Jack to safety. Although Cipher was known to keep a calm head under stress, she felt herself drifting precariously toward abject despair.

Deep breath, Cipher, she told herself. *Remember your training.*

"Good to see you, Marissa," said a deep voice behind her, in English. It was a harmonious tone, roughened by cigarettes and alcohol.

She turned back around to see a man in an ivory-colored *shalwar* and maroon *pagri*—a compact turban, whose long end had been dropped to the throat and wrapped around as a loose scarf. His face was the color of bronze only seen on statues and hearty souls who had spent years sailing the Indian Ocean and Arabian Sea, and it carried the scars of a thousand brutal conflicts. A small, well-trimmed Van Dyke beard of jet black graced his pointed chin, and two warm brown eyes peered out from beneath a red, hand-painted *bindi.*

Cipher couldn't believe her eyes. "R-Rajiv?" she stammered.

The wiry man smiled. "I would never speak for you, of course," he said, "but it appears that you could use some help."

∞

Charlie "Deadeye" Dalton was known for being able to sleep on demand, in the most uncomfortable of environments, in the most difficult of situations. He'd taken cat naps on the Western Front during bombing raids and artillery barrages. He'd eked out twenty winks in the hold of a tramp steamer in a hurricane while crossing the Atlantic. And he was famous for snoozing away while strapped into a gun turret on a light recon airship. Lounging in the morning sun atop the outer envelope of the *Daedalus* was neither uncomfortable nor difficult.

Of course, he never went radio silent when on duty, so the two-piece AEGIS field radio lay by his head, and his trusty M1903 Springfield rifle, with its shiny new Zeiss telescopic sight, lay under the blanket to his right.

The sudden *pop* of far-off gunfire woke him from his nap, and Deadeye immediately sat up, scanning the distance. The vantage from atop the dorsal envelope of the airship was akin to that of a ten-story building, and he could easily see across the rail terminus into the marketplace, where locals were screaming and scattering in colorful chaos. As he reached for his rifle under the blanket, the radio erupted in a barrage of beeping.

G-U-N-M-A-N / 2-N-D-S-T-O-R-E-Y / E-S-P-L-A-N-A-D-E / N-N-W / N-E-E-D-S-U-P-P-O-R-T //

The Morse code *dits* and *dahs* came chirping over the wireless. Deadeye reached toward the radio and tapped out a quick reply on the key: . _ ., or *R* for "received".

He folded the two halves of the radio together, latching them in place to form a square box. Shifting it a few inches to his left, he draped the second blanket over it before laying the barrel stock of the rifle on top of the makeshift mount. Peering through the eyepiece of the scope, he delicately adjusted the distance and focus, performing subtle calculations in his head to adjust for wind, distance, and the lazy drift of the *Daedalus* at her mooring cables.

Charlie swallowed, but his spit had gone dry. The market was a chaotic mess. There were already dead bodies on the ground. As he scanned through the scope for any sign of his crewmates, he saw the line of agents approaching the open square, and it dawned on him how much trouble they were actually in.

◯&

Doc tried desperately to keep her wits, but was almost completely lost in panic. Every time she moved, another burst from the BAR across the street erupted near her, kicking up shards of cobblestone and splinters of wood from the produce carts. The square had cleared of pedestrians, creating a focused line of fire for the gunman. Though she was in great shape, there was no way she could carry Jack's unconscious form anywhere resembling safety. And then there was the poison factor. He'd luckily only received a scratch, not the full blade penetration the poor civilian woman had suffered, but she had no idea what kind of toxin it was, how quickly it would kill him, or how to counteract it.

It was like her late husband all over again.

With tears streaming unabated from her green eyes, Doc grabbed Jack and held him close, tracking his labored breathing and accelerating heartbeat. That at least had the effect of pulling her into a clinical frame of mind, where she could more comfortably deal with stressful situations like the one in which they found themselves. Pulling open Jack's left eyelid, then the right, she noted the pupils contracted with exposure to sunlight. That was something close to good news in the midst of horror.

The gunfire stopped abruptly, and Doc peeked over the top of the shattered cart to see a line of local Silver Star cohorts approaching the square. There was surely no escape now. Not with Jack in tow, anyway.

Doc set her jaw and steeled herself, either for their inevitable capture—or Jack's if she made a run for it—and suddenly Cipher skidded to a halt beside her.

"What the—?"

"Here to help, ma'am," Cipher reported, using the British pronunciation *mom*.

The small, wiry man in the maroon turban appeared from behind the cart to their right, rushing to Doc's side and kneeling by Jack. He listened to the wounded man's halting breath, then the thrumming heartbeat that threatened to burst from his chest. He saw the wash of blood down Jack's left arm, and looked over the wound.

"Was it a throwing blade?" he asked Doc.

"Yes," she blinked, "poisoned, I assume, but I'm not sure what—"

"It's a highly toxic alkaloid—derived from the *tambaku* plant—we have minutes at best."

Doc squinted through her clinical brain fog. "Wait, what? Who are—?"

"This is Rajiv," Cipher answered, resting a calm hand on Doc's shoulder. "He's a friend."

Doc nodded. "Fine, swell we've got to get Jack to safety. If you two can carry him, I'll try to hold off the incoming agents. Get him back to the *Daedalus* as quickly as you can." She suddenly wished she had more than just her revolver and Jack's .45 at hand.

Cipher put up a hand in protest. "But ma'am, you're the doctor! Shouldn't you go with the captain?"

"My ship is closer in the harbor," Rajiv interrupted. "And my surgeon is familiar with this type of poison." The bronze man reached back and unslung a Thompson submachine gun that had been hiding behind his billowy clothing. "Can you fire one of these?" he asked Doc.

Dorothy Starr blinked again, the fog clearing, her wits returning. "Absolutely," she said with authority.

"Very good," Rajiv grinned, showing off a gleaming gold tooth where his upper left canine should have been. "Marissa, you and I will each take a side. When we go, we don't stop until we get him to my ship. He can be treated, but we must hurry."

Doc ratcheted back the bolt on the Tommy gun. "Let's go already," she hissed through sun-chapped lips.

They stood as one, Rajiv and Cipher hoisting Jack between them, each ducking under an arm and taking hold of his field belt from behind. Doc hefted the Tommy gun and flipped the safety switch forward to fire, noting the secondary switch was already set to full auto.

Instantly, the gunman in the window across the Esplanade opened up with the BAR, blasting chunks of cobblestone and dirt, while the line of turbaned agents proceeded forward under his fire arc.

A single shot echoed across the market square from behind Doc, and she barely caught the rupture of a pane of glass. The BAR fell silent, then tumbled from the balcony to the street below. *Thank you, Charlie!* she thought, planting her stance to cover the getaway of Rajiv, Cipher, and the unconscious Jack.

As her index finger squeezed the trigger, the Tommy gun began to buck and kick, spitting 45-caliber rounds across the square. Its roar was like that of a dragon in her ears, and she could feel the heat from the barrel as it ceaselessly breathed fire at the encroaching gunmen. Two men fell instantly, their bodies beginning to smoke and bubble. It was something they'd seen repeatedly in their many encounters with agents of the Silver Star. The souls promised to Crowley as collateral were being called in.

The others opened fire with their own weapons, and at that moment Doc wished dearly she hadn't left the Athenian vambrace aboard the *Daedalus*. A gift from AEGIS benefactor Marina Stavros, the forearm plate could be invoked to create a mystical bubble of energy around the wearer, a shield against incoming attack. But it was one hundred percent non-effective while sitting on the table next to the bunk in her quarters.

She squatted down behind the wooden cart, feeling the wakes of a dozen rounds whiz past her head. Lucky. Very lucky. If she continued to be this lucky, by the law of averages, she might survive a second try at the gunmen before they got her for good. But at least it would buy the precious time necessary to get Jack to safety and treat the poison. She wouldn't get the opportunity to bid farewell to her love, or to their daughter, Ellen. But there were letters in a safety deposit box in West Orange for that. She swallowed, bracing herself to receive the bullets with her name on them.

Then she stood, spraying the square with hot metal. The gunmen fired back.

The machine gun roared, kicking in her hands. A third man fell, and a fourth. Three men remained.

Doc's arms ached, from shoulders to fingertips, but she continued to fire. An enemy round struck her in the left shoulder. Another the left thigh. She felt the flesh split in a fountain of blood and cotton fibers.

As Doc watched, the gunman on the left end fell, the report of a single rifle shot echoing from behind her. That left two.

One of the last two fell as his head erupted in a red spray. Once again, she heard the rifle shot reach her ears from behind.

That left the last gunman—

The 1925 Vauxhall four-seater came roaring off the Esplanade like a silver shark, skidding to the side as it collided with the remaining Silver Star agent, folding the man in half. His weapon rolled and skittered away toward the Market Road, his body beginning to disintegrate before it hit the cobblestones. The driver recovered from the spin, revving the engine toward Doc and the perforated produce cart.

Doc's right arm spasmed and she realized she was still holding the trigger down. The Tommy gun had run out of ammo from the long stick magazine some seconds ago. The car barreled toward her, and she dropped to a defensive squat, preparing to spring out of the way at the last moment.

The driver slammed on the brakes, tires screaming to a halt on the fruit-strewn pavement barely two feet from her.

"Going my way, love?" Duke asked, flashing his charming grin.

Doc limped around to the passenger side and fell into the red leather seat next to him, tossing the Thompson into the back. Duke noticed that people were starting to peek out of the Market building and probe the square once again. He knew the authorities would find only empty clothing, piles of ash and bone fragments, and weapons they could trace no further than the black market.

"Where's Jack?" he asked, throwing the Vauxhall into gear and peeling out in a southerly heading.

"Cipher and...a friend. Dragging him to the docks. He's been poisoned. Hopefully they made the Terminus by now."

As she said "made the Terminus," the car tires bumping and bobbling over a set of rail tracks near the harbor, the lumbering forms of Cipher, Rajiv, and Jack came into view. They'd cleared the last rail line and were headed toward a nearby pier, where a questionable-looking tramp steamer was moored. The car no longer necessary, Duke pulled to a stop and killed the engine. "Shall we?" he nodded.

They climbed from the silver sports car and Duke went to look Doc over. Her left arm hung slack at her side, and she limped on her left leg. Both limbs were awash in dark red. "Oh dear," he frowned. "We should get these seen to."

Doc suddenly felt very hot, as if she'd walked into a steam bath by mistake. She nodded, breath heavy in her chest. Then she collapsed, unconscious, into Duke's arms.

- CHAPTER 6 -

A casual passerby might have mistaken the *Kali* for merely an ancient rust bucket, barely seaworthy, but such an assumption would only be partially correct. A German AK-5 class transport from the African front during the Great War, she'd been refitted as many times as she'd been around the Cape of Good Hope and back. Captained by the dashing Rajiv and manned by reprobates from every port of call in Asia and Africa, she looked far older and worse for wear than her twenty-five years in service, but somehow managed to remain afloat and mobile. In fact, even with her leaky 800-horsepower diesel engine and single screw, she was known to hit eight knots on a good day. How that was possible, nobody thought to question. Like the sunset, or the tides, or the summer monsoon, it simply was.

A lacquer Gennett record rotated quietly on the phonograph in the corner of the sick bay, trilling the jazz strains of Hoagy Carmichael's new hit, "Stardust", through the speaker horn. A steel hospital cot occupied each of the starboard interior and port hull walls. The unconscious Jack McGraw took up one, Doc the other, in a similar state of unconsciousness.

The ship's surgeon was an ancient Maylaysian the crew called Dr. Mamat. He was a stooped-over five-foot-four with a deep tan, stark white beard, and leathery complexion. His spindly arms were almost impossibly veiny under their parchment-like skin, quite resembling the coiled, spiraling tubes of his homemade blood transfusion machine. A rusty metal work counter in the ramshackle infirmary was littered with the tools of his trade: bloodstained gauze pads, aluminum kidney pans filled with scissors and scalpels, and a well-used mortar and pestle smeared with the residue of an old folk remedy—the antidote that would save Jack's life. If they were lucky.

While the herbal poultice smeared copiously on Jack's arm did its work and the transfusion machine pumped away, Dr. Mamat turned his attention to Doc, gingerly suturing her wounds and rolling gauze around her arm and leg. As he worked, he hummed along to the record.

Duke stood in the yellow battery light of the infirmary and rubbed at the inside of his elbow, where Mamat had spiked it to procure the blood donation. He glanced over at Rajiv, who leaned against the wall by the door. "I say, old man, it's lucky you were in port."

The captain nodded to various corners of the room within the old tramp freighter, raising an eyebrow as he did so. "The *Kali* is my home," he said. "But Mumbai is hers." He flashed a bold smile. "I'm glad too. When I checked in with the field office last night, they warned me of an increased Silver Star presence in the city. They definitely knew you were here."

"We're...em...'high-profile' targets for the Astrum Argentum," Duke admitted.

"I imagine so, especially in those airships of yours."

Duke smiled. "The light recon ships are versatile, but not nearly as impressive as the supercarriers employed by the Silver Star."

"Most of our interactions with that lot have been on the land or at sea," Rajiv noted. "And that's been adventure enough."

"How long have you been with AEGIS?" Duke asked.

"Since last year," the captain answered. "Sir Harold Marston recruited me in Africa. He knew a rusty freighter running the Indian Ocean would be an intelligence resource, and a good way to move assets without attracting attention." He cast a thoughtful look at the metal floor for a moment, then added, "And the job has had some perks." For the first time, Duke noticed the light gleam off a couple golden teeth in the left side of the Indian's smile.

"Well, my thanks again, Captain," Duke nodded, bowing slightly. "We owe you."

Rajiv chuckled, clapping Duke on the shoulder as he exited the infirmary. "I know," he winked.

As the transfusion machine huffed away like an asthmatic hiker, Rajiv left the sick bay, stepping out into the dimly-lit corridor.

Cipher was waiting for him, leaning against the wall, holding her scuffed and stained service beret in her hand.

"Marissa," he startled, "I—"

She leaned in close and kissed him, pressing her lips passionately to his. "Thank you," she said softly, pulling away.

Rajiv kept his composure, though his face was a mask of amused surprise. "I'm sorry I didn't write. When you left, all I could find out was that you had joined the Royal Army. I thought I'd lost you to the Empire."

"I was recruited into AEGIS from communications training. And let us not speak of the Empire. I have come to have questions of my own."

Rajiv let out a contented sigh and wrapped Cipher in his arms. She returned the embrace, tears glistening in her red-rimmed eyes. It lasted only a few brief moments before the *Kali*'s radioman came stomping down the hallway, paper in hand.

"Captain!" the slender Ethiopian hailed. "Encrypted orders for airships *Daedalus* and *Percival*."

"Thank you, Amahl," Rajiv nodded. "Return to your station and keep listening for further transmissions."

Out of propriety, Cipher waited for the radioman to hand the paper to Rajiv and make his exit before grabbing it to read herself. "The key is correct," she mused, scanning the lines of gibberish. "And it's signed 'Mr. Vagabond', which is Edison."

"Yes, I've been meaning to ask about that..." Rajiv said, pursing his lips.

"Edison, Ford, Firestone," Cipher said matter-of-factly. "The Vagabonds."

The captain's forehead wrinkled in confusion. His command of English wasn't perfect, but he knew what "vagabond" meant, and it wasn't a word he'd associate with wealthy American industrialists. It occurred to him that the name was probably self-given and ironic, and he let it go at that.

Suddenly Deadeye appeared at the far end of the corridor, flanked by a crewman with a sidearm. "Cipher," he called. "Did you get the message too?" He strode with purpose to Cipher and Rajiv. "Charlie Dalton of the airship *Daedalus*," he announced, giving Rajiv a quick salute.

Rajiv returned the gesture and did a double-take. "'Deadeye' Dalton?" he wondered aloud. "You're sort of a legend, you know. And if that was your marksmanship covering our escape at the market, it's a legend well deserved. Name's Rajiv, Captain of the *Kali*." he offered his hand, and Deadeye shook it firmly.

"I'd love to chat, Captain, but we have urgent orders. What's the condition of Captain McGraw and Doctor Starr?"

Rajiv opened his mouth to reply, and a voice came from behind him.

"Alive...thanks to Captain Rajiv and Dr. Mamat, and you, Charlie...again." Jack McGraw stood braced in the infirmary doorway, pale and clammy. Sweat beaded on his forehead and purple bags hung under his eyes.

He looked as bad as he ever had, thought Deadeye.

Cipher turned with a gasp. "Captain, you're awake!"

"Apparently," said Jack, smacking his lips dryly. "What's this about orders?"

Deadeye handed Jack a folded piece of paper from the *Daedalus'* radio station. "It took us about ten minutes to decode with the key at the ship. I was just seeing if Cipher had also received—"

"Received and decoded on the fly, sir," Cipher nodded. "Silver Star activity reported in Bangkok, Siam. At least one of their supercarriers sighted over the city."

There was a pause, while Jack blinked and tried to reconcile the spoken words with the written ones on Deadeye's note. His world was still a bit wobbly—and being on board a ship in the water wasn't helping that—but the transmission made sense. It was the general route they were following anyway. He just wished he knew which of the two colossal dirigibles was carrying their captive mechanic, Rivets.

"Very well then," Jack grunted, using all of his strength to remain upright and avoid collapsing in the doorway. "Let's tie up our affairs here in Bombay and chart a flight plan for Siam."

Rajiv lowered his gaze to the floor, regretting what he knew would be Cipher's imminent departure.

❧

Rivets grunted as the aluminum brig door slid open. He rested horizontally on a metal cot too small for his wide frame, facing the wall. The reverberations of the *Luftpanzer*'s massive diesel engines, coupled with the poor air filtration in the brig, created an environment more suitable for sleeping than anything requiring actual thought or activity.

He'd lost count of the days; his world had become an eight-foot-by-eight-foot cell where the soporific drone of engines was interrupted twice a day for meager meals and a ration of water. His waste went into what literally appeared to be a medical bedpan welded to a wall strut, connected to a flexible hose that drained everything out of sight and mind.

Life before his capture was a jumble of foggy memories. The torture probably had something to do with it. He remembered resisting for the first few days as his captors attempted various methods of gaining his compliance. It had pushed him right up to the edge of "too much to bear", and he'd fed them some old intelligence under the guise of "breaking". At least it had put a stop to the pain for a while.

They'd put him in the infirmary to recover, and now he was back in his cell to await the day when they'd come to take him to laboratory with the captured dynamo, and show them how it worked—how everything worked.

"Commander Holloway," said an officious male voice tinged with a British accent. "Wake up."

Rivets grunted again and turned over far enough to see a slender young crewman with close-cropped dark hair peering at him from the open cell door. "Come back tomorrow," he growled. "I'm busy."

"I should inform you, Commander, that I've been authorized by *Kommandant* Blutig herself to employ whatever methods necessary to get you to the laboratory this afternoon for your little demonstration." Rivets gave no reply, and the young agent cleared his throat before continuing. "I should also remind the Commander that those very methods put him in the ship's infirmary for three days straight."

"Jesus, Mary, and Joseph, you sure can blather." Rivets swung his feet to the floor and sat upright. "Fine. Take me to the lab."

He stood, right leg still sore from where he'd been struck by an enemy machine gun round over two weeks ago. Although Doc had dug it out and sewn the wound shut, Rivets' captors had spent some time and focus on the wound during his first days of torment. It now pulsed with chronic pain and gave him a sorry limp.

The young agent gestured, and two armed soldiers stepped forward. One produced a set of manacles and locked Rivets' hands in front of him.

"I dunno, boys," Rivets quipped. "Do you have anything in a 46 regular?"

He'd barcly finished the sentence when the butt of an MP-18 submachine gun impacted his ribs, knocking the breath from his lungs. He collapsed to his knees, gasping and choking.

The young agent approached him with a calm assurance. "Commander Holloway, are you going to cooperate, or do we need to send you back to the infirmary after proper... motivation?"

"No motivation," Rivets coughed. "I'm motivated."

Each guard grabbed an arm, hauling Rivets back to his feet. They marched him from the brig, with the young agent following behind.

Though he appeared dazed, Rivets pretended much of his infirmity, taking in every detail of the trip from the brig to the laboratory. He noted the brig was aft, just forward of the main cargo hold. He counted six engine rooms as they moved toward the nose of the giant airship, three on each side. That meant the Silver Star were still tending their giant diesel engines individually, the old fashioned way.

He counted eighty-seven paces from the brig to the door of the laboratory. As they paused to await permission to enter, a quick glance down from the gantry through one of the angled portholes below told Rivets they were over tropical blue water and a stretch of verdant green island. He estimated their altitude at perhaps 5,000 feet, and guessed their location somewhere in the South Pacific.

A stern female voice hailed from inside the lab, and the young agent opened the door. Rivets entered, flanked by the armed guards. The agent followed the trio inside, shutting the door behind them. The room was a simple utility laboratory, with aluminum work benches on the fore and aft walls. A work table of similar construction, but half again wider, took up the center. The interior was bleached in sickly yellow incandescent light from the wall fixtures.

"Hello, Commander Holloway," purred a familiar voice from the far end of the room. It was tinged with a German accent and the hint of a cultivated, barely-contained rage. The woman stepped forward into the bilious light and revealed to Rivets her identity: Maria Blutig, "Bloody Mary", the She-Wolf of the Astrum Argentum. Tall and slender, clad in the charcoal gray officer's uniform of the Silver Star, Maria's icy blue eyes peered out from under the raven-black bob hugging her pale face. She held an officer's swagger stick tucked under her left arm, but it was nothing like the batons carried by the British officers in the trenches of the Western Front; this implement was carved in an intricate spiral of ancient runes and pictograms. Rivets didn't know much about the occult side of the AEGIS mission, but he'd been privy to some unusual experiences during his tenure in the organization, and he thought that stick looked very much like something a mage might use as a spell focus, or a wand.

"Heya, toots," Rivets grunted. "It's been too long...or not long enough."

Maria smiled as a cat stalking a small rodent. "Guards, remove his chains."

One of the soldiers unlocked the manacles and removed the chains from the mechanic's wrists. He rubbed them convincingly.

"Commander," Maria began, "under ordinary circumstances, we would have taken the dynamo to one of our research facilities in Europe to be disassembled and reverse-engineered." She paced the floor grates in knee-high officer's boots, each step a reverberating *clop*. "Because of our current mission parameters, we are forced to delay such a plan. However, we do have someone right here, on this ship, who can save us much time and expense."

"Now why would I want to save either of those things for you?" Rivets chuckled.

Maria flashed a look across the table at the young agent. "Agent M-625, contact the *Osiris* and see if *Herr* Himmler requires any assistance with his experiment."

The young agent snapped briefly to attention, then exited without a further word.

With another look, Maria directed the two armed guards to step back. Both unshouldered their weapons, holding them at the ready.

"Now, Commander," she smiled that familiar predatory smile, "I want you to show me how the dynamo functions."

Rivets leaned forward, resting his fists on the work table. "Why the rush, doll? Why not wait and have your boys take it apart?" He raised an eyebrow. "Unless you're not sure they *can*..."

"I understand your resistance to giving us a working knowledge of your dynamo generator technology," Maria said softly, tapping the wide end of the swagger stick with a manicured fingernail. "But you simply have no choice in the matter."

Rivets folded his two massive arms across his chest. "Oh I don't, do I?"

Suddenly the wand was in her hand, and Rivets felt an overwhelming blankness fill his mind.

"No," Maria said matter-of-factly. "No, you don't."

Rivets staggered in place at the table. The room began to tilt and split into several different versions of itself. His head felt like an angry beehive, his body somehow not his own. He knew he had to show Maria the dynamo's inner workings, but he wasn't sure why. He steadied himself against the table's edge and reached for the captured generator.

- CHAPTER 7 -

Rajiv had not been boasting when he called Bombay *Kali*'s home. The captain was incredibly well-connected, and within a few hour's time, a small army of contacts had been mobilized throughout the city, procuring food and gathering the items on Dhakiya's list.

Doc regained consciousness long enough to prescribe a protein-vitamin compound for Jack and herself, then the two of them returned to the *Daedalus* and collapsed in their respective bunks. It was the first time Jack hadn't personally overseen a provision loadout and systems check prior to departure, but he trusted Cipher and Deadeye to handle the details, and Duke to oversee the operation on behalf of both ships. Asim and Dhakiya, too, had proved themselves able and competent crew members at the very least. Heck, he was alive that day because he'd placed his trust in these people, and they'd come through, very much as it had been in the Great War.

Cipher met Rajiv on the dock near the *Kali*'s gangplank. She'd changed into a fresh set of clothes and her hair was re-braided. "I cannot thank you enough, Rajiv. On behalf of my captain—"

"It was good to see you again, Marissa," Rajiv interjected. "I am glad your captain will recover. But now old Dr. Mamat will want a rise in pay."

Cipher smiled warmly. "I'm sure if you submit a report with the field office in Delhi, you will be compensated."

The two stood on the dock, radiant chestnut eyes staring at each other. Cipher could hear the *Kali*'s diesel engine churn to life. The rusty freighter and her crew would depart at the same time as the two AEGIS airships, under cover of early morning darkness. Rajiv was overdue in Cairo, and his ship heading the opposite direction of the *Daedalus* and *Percival* would add some confusion to any attempts by the Silver Star to follow them.

"Be careful," Rajiv warned. "Our enemy is not to be underestimated."

Cipher blushed. "That is a lesson already learned."

"You were always the more attentive student." Rajiv leaned forward, meeting Cipher in a farewell kiss. They lingered for a moment, and as his lips departed hers, he whispered in her ear. "*Triśūla.*"

She puzzled for a moment, then understood. *Triśūla.* Punjabi for *trident.* He'd given her a keyword.

"Send that on your lowest frequency," he instructed, "and I will come to your aid, with all haste."

With the humid night still glistening on her bullet-shaped envelope, the *Daedalus* rose into the dark sky over Bombay. The *Percival* followed her, winding a course east-southeast over the Indian subcontinent. At the same time, the *Kali* disengaged from Alexandra dock and left the harbor, steaming full speed to the west across the Arabian Sea.

CB

Rivets wasn't a naturally clumsy man, by any stretch of the imagination, nor was he an actor. So when he pretended to trip on his own feet, falling to all fours, the effort was somewhat less than convincing, despite putting every mental effort into resisting Maria's mind control. He launched the uncovered dynamo into the air, and it shattered against the bulkhead. Aluminum gears clattered onto the deckplate, and the primary flywheel rolled like a warped phonograph record to the corner of the room, where it made contact with the wall and fell on its side. Hand-blown vacuum tubes were reduced to tiny shards of crystalline-looking glass.

A Silver Star soldier was on Rivets instantly, clutching him by the back of his coveralls and pressing the barrel of a 9mm pistol into his neck.

"Stop!" Maria ordered. Her catlike expression displayed no shock at Rivets' action, only a slight disappointment at that the next stage of natural consequences would have to follow.

"Damn," Rivets huffed from his position on the floor. "I think it might be busted."

The soldier looked up at Maria in disbelief. She blinked slowly, and he shoved Rivets down, backing away, but keeping the pistol trained on him.

Maria began to laugh, and it was the sound of genuine amusement. "Oh, Commander," she smiled with predatory ease, "the dynamo means nothing to us." She surveyed the hunched form of the mechanic on the floor as he slowly staggered to his feet. "This was merely the first test of many."

Rivets winced as he put weight on his wounded leg. He squinted across the room constructed of perforated aluminum struts and vulcanized canvas at the woman in the black uniform, and his eyes widened with a realization. "You weren't after the dynamo at all."

Maria laughed with the delight of watching a child perform. "No, of course not." She shook her head, still chuckling. "Edison and his ego. My technicians had already disassembled and diagrammed the dynamo long before you were brought here. But we have no *need* for your puny reactionless motor, when we are in possession of far more powerful technology."

"Then what do you want?" Rivets muttered.

"It's you, Commander Holloway, and what's in your mind." Maria tapped her right temple with the silver tip of her swagger stick, and it sent a shiver down Rivets' spine. "We needed to gauge how cooperative you would be after your first round of...'softening'. Clearly you are not yet ready to share what I want to know."

"Know?" Rivets grunted. "Know about what?"

Maria's eyes glowed in the dim light of the room, mocking him, searing his brain. "About AEGIS...about their structure and mission plans...and about Captain Jack McGraw."

Rivets' felt his stomach sink as if he'd inverted in a barrel roll. They weren't about to let him off with a simple bullet to the head. They wanted far more from him than a technology primer. If there was a safe harbor from the storm, he was far from it.

"Take him back to his cell," Maria ordered coldly. "We'll start again tomorrow."

The soldier shoved Rivets from behind, and this time he stumbled for real. Grabbed once again by the back of the coveralls and wrestled toward the door, Rivets struggled to meet Maria's gaze.

"N-no matter what I tell you," he huffed, "Jack won't fall for any tricks. My pals...they know exactly who—and *what*—you are."

Maria approached uncomfortably closely, her face mere inches from his. She inhaled the delightful smell of fear from his bushy mustache. "Get some rest, Commander Holloway. You've got a rough day ahead."

Then she was gone from the room, stalking away presumably on some other villainous business, and he was manhandled back to the brig and shoved into his cell. Curling into a fetal position on the wire bunk, Rivets began to weep silently. All he could feel was abject terror. Terror not of the impending torture, but what harm might befall his friends from any knowledge gleaned from him under further duress. So far, he'd endured. But his strength would not hold out forever.

He just wished Jack and the crew would get there and bust him out already.

❦

The flight plan called for a crossing of 1,145 miles, roughly seventeen hours at a cruising speed of seventy miles per hour. It would take the two small airships over the jungles and villages of the Indian interior, the sprawling Bay of Bengal, and the narrow tail of Burma. They also had to account for traveling in the height of monsoon season. A formidable headwind had other plans for them, pushing against the airships with every nautical mile. Although capable of top speeds of one hundred miles per hour, with each ship lacking a dynamo generator, they dared not push the engines so hard. Their estimated seventeen hours only took them as far as the northern point of the Andaman Islands, fighting for every mile. Just after 10 p.m., the summer storm behind the headwind decided to come out and play.

Jack awoke to thunder over the Bay of Bengal. The air in his quarters was hot, and stank of stale sweat and salt air. With a weary grunt, he pushed himself upright and staggered away from his bunk, bracing himself in the doorway as he fumbled with the latch. The airship's frame shook and jostled in a gust of wind. No way was he going to sleep through this. He pushed open the door and stepped from his tiny stateroom to find Doc directing the crew like a veteran symphony conductor.

"Keep her nose up, Asim," she barked from the bridge hatchway. "I'll be right back."

Still a bit wobbly on his feet, especially given the ever-increasing air turbulence, Jack staggered to meet her as she crossed the main saloon toward the engine room. "What's cookin'?" he quipped.

"Picked up a storm coming in off the Burma Sea. We need some more altitude and some extra power to the engines. I was just heading back to see if I could help Dhakiya." Doc leaned in and gave Jack a quick peck on the cheek. "You look better," she smiled.

"I feel like I've been hit by a truck," Jack replied. "But that's never stopped me before. I'll come with you."

Jack was gratified to see Doc in such remarkably good shape. She still sported a thick cotton bandage around her left thigh, another anchored to the front of her shoulder with a criss cross of gauze. She was usually the one digging bullets out of the crew, but Jack found himself trying to remember if she'd ever taken a round before. She'd served as a battlefield nurse on the Western Front, hip-deep in mud, blood, and severed limbs. She'd been around the world, fighting the Silver Star and its well-armed soldiers. The Amazon. The Himalayas. Africa. Was this really her first time getting hit by gunfire?

They moved past the aft belly hatch and Doc opened the door to the engine room. "Dhakiya?" she hailed. "Here to lend a hand."

The Kenyan mechanic was clad in her roughed up khaki trousers and cuffed work shirt, a pair of protective goggles sitting atop her brow. She stood at the workbench, leaning over what appeared to be one of the eight remaining dynamos, disconnected from the other generators and missing its tempered glass housing.

Jack scowled. With only eight generators functioning, no wonder they were struggling against the approaching storm! "Say, what's the big idea?"

"It's almost ready," Dhakiya murmured. "Just aligning the last magnet..."

Doc recognized a kind of genius at work. "What can we do?" she asked.

"Stand back," said the mechanic, lowering the goggles over her eyes. "I'm going to reconnect the dynamo to the array. When I tell you, switch the circuit on, but keep a hand on the bypass in case it overloads. I'm not entirely sure what its output will be."

Jack knew in theory what she was talking about, but had no practical idea how to comply.

"What's the matter, Captain? Don't know your own ship?" Doc chuckled, stepping over to the electrical panel full of gauges and switches. She noted that the No. 9 circuit was in the *OFF* position.

Dhakiya cradled the reconfigured dynamo in work-worn hands. The ship rumbled with another buffet of storm wind, and Jack winced as she staggered off balance, recovering her footing at the far end of the generator bay. The previous *Daedalus* powerplant had sported eight DiMarco-Edison Mark 3 reactionless gyroscopes. Whereas the new ship was initially outfitted with ten Mark 4 dynamos, only eight currently functioned. Dhakiya gingerly lowered her cannibalized generator into the No. 9 bay, pinching a cable between her fingers and fitting the connector to the plug in the dynamo's metal housing. She inserted her index finger into the open top of the cylinder, where a linked series of rotors and gimbals were stacked on an aluminum axle of sorts. Jack could see a number of small magnets secured to the rotors and the inside of the cylinder, and suddenly the the entire concept washed over him. The Mk 4 dynamos required restarting every twenty-four hours, using a ripcord to set the central rotors spinning. She'd rigged the gyroscope with magnets to run continuously, without ever slowing or winding down. The gimbals and central rotors had become a perpetual turbine. She'd almost completely reinvented the ship's power source.

"Get ready," said the young engineer, nudging the top flywheel in a clockwise spin. "Turn on the circuit."

Doc switched the No. 9 circuit to the *ON* position, watching with Jack as the rotors picked up speed, sending the gimbals whipping around in a tiny cyclone, urged ever faster by the specific polarity of the magnets in the housing. Faster and faster they spun. Doc checked the power gauge on the No. 9 circuit and watched the level steadily increase. Her right hand felt for the red *BYPASS* button on the console and hovered over it, ready for the worst.

A brief plume of sparks shot up from the generator's housing, framing Dhakiya's goggled face in flickering white light, making her appear as some kind of female Dr. Frankenstein. She reached below the generator bay and produced a cylindrical glass dome cover, placing it carefully over the top of the spinning turbine as tendrils of electricity arced and flexed over the housing.

The power level continued to climb: fifty kilowatts.

Sixty.

Seventy.

"Eighty kilowatts," Doc reported, as Jack stared wide-eyed at the spinning generator, and Dhakiya angled her face away from any potential short-circuit reaction. She was in her element, focused intently on the experiment.

Jack glanced at the power gauge at the monitor console. "Ninety…"

Dhakiya turned to look over her shoulder at the power gauge on the console. As the needle hit one hundred kilowatts, she turned back to the powerplant, squinting through the goggles. "The circuit can only handle a hundred twenty kilowatts. If it passes one ten, kill it."

The ship thumped and shook in another storm gust, and the three suddenly felt themselves get heavier as the *Daedalus* surged higher. The increase in thruster RPMs vibrated through the gondola walls.

"One hundred five," Doc warned.

Dhakiya held up a finger. "Steady," she said calmly, still peering through the tinted lenses.

"One ten! Should I hit the bypass?"

"Stand by," the engineer replied, her single warning finger becoming an open hand.

The three stood swaying in the engine room as the increasing storm winds lashed the envelope outside. The whine of the ship's electrical systems and the giant outboard thrusters hummed through the perforated metal deckplates.

Dhakiya stared at the whirring dynamo next to her, pushing the goggles back to rest on her forehead. "What's it reading now?"

Doc read the gauge, blinking. "Holding steady at one hundred ten," she said.

Dhakiya smiled. "Good," she muttered, more to herself than to anyone in the room. "Very good."

"I should say so," Jack marveled. "Do you know what you've done?"

Dhakiya looked blankly at the tall pilot. She wasn't sure if she should prepare for praise or a dressing-down. She was mostly used to the latter from the British aviators at the Mombasa airfield.

Jack extended a hand, clapping the young airplane mechanic on the shoulder. His ears felt like they were packed with cotton, and he swallowed to equalize the pressure. Suddenly he felt himself craving a stick of his licorice chewing gum. "You've just upgraded the entire AEGIS aerofleet," he grinned. "And quite probably saved our bacon."

Dhakiya flashed a brief smile and blushed, her eyes downcast. She wasn't used to compliments. "Happy to help."

"Will the *Percival* be able to get beyond the storm as well?" Doc worried.

Jack shrugged. "They can alter course and fly around it, if necessary. Duke knows his business."

Doc nodded in agreement. "Alright then," she said. "We should get back to the bridge, give Asim some guidance navigating the storm." She patted the engineer on the back, adding, "This is big, Dhakiya." Then she stepped out of the engine room and was gone.

Jack turned to Dhakiya and shook his head in disbelief. "I still can't believe what you were able to do with a few magnets." Making his way to the engine room door, he pushed it open and paused while straddling the threshold. "I owe you. We all do. You've got one heck of a future ahead you, Sparks."

- CHAPTER 8 -

Jack and Doc arrived on the bridge just as a bolt of lightning arced across the sky, deceptively close to the windscreens. The ship rattled and jumped, buffeted by the relentless wind. Every flash in the black and angry sky resembled bursting artillery in a twisting cloud of smoke. Despite their altitude and the magnitude of the storm, the cabin remained sultry. Doc dialed down the bridge thermostat; it would draw less power.

As Jack approached the pilot's station, Asim saw him and began to unfasten his safety harness. Jack could see he was several shades paler than his normal complexion, undoubtedly due to the fact that he'd never flown in anything but calm weather.

Laying a hand on Asim's shoulder, he reassured the young pilot. "Keep your station, Lieutenant," he instructed. "I'm out of gum." Pointing to a power gauge on the pilot's console, he added, "Our engineer has rigged a few more kilowatts for us. Throttle up to ninety miles per hour and dump all ballast to climb."

Cipher turned in her seat at the comms station. She remembered Jack's gambit back in April, when he pushed the *Daedalus* beyond her official specs to outclimb the Silver Star fighter planes pestering them over Europe. They'd ended up ascending to 28,000 feet. But if he was thinking along similar lines, there was no way they'd be able to get over this particular storm. Not if her last radio detector readings were to be believed. "Captain, the system has an absolute cloud top of over 52,000 feet."

"Don't worry, Cipher," Jack said, keeping his focus on the pilot's console and the petrified Asim. "We're not going over it. We're going to come about and use that headwind as a tailwind. We're going ride it like a carousel."

Cipher found herself exhaling in relief. Granted, if they had to fly through a storm, there was no one she'd want more at the stick than Captain Stratosphere. Just the same, she'd prefer not to fly through the storm in the first place.

"Contact the *Percival*," Jack ordered. "Tell them to keep a radio reading on us and follow our lead as best they can. If we get separated, rendezvous in Bangkok when feasible."

Cipher turned back to her console to comply, noting a sudden burst of radio chatter in German and English in the band to which she kept her receiver tuned to pick up Silver Star communications. In the midst of the garbled static, a string of Morse code was plain: *D-Y-N-A-M-O / K-A-P-U-T*. Making a mental note to inform the captain when his attention wasn't on the immediate danger in front of them, she patched a cord into the two-way radio system and contacted the *Percival*.

Doc finished rolling up one of her charts, slipping it into a thick cardboard tube and sliding it into a cubby hole to her right. She wanted to make sure there was nothing loose at the nav station when things got shaky. And she knew they would get shaky.

As Cipher repeated Jack's instructions into her station microphone, Jack leaned over Asim and spoke in an easy, fatherly tone.

"What's our speed?"

"N-ninety," Asim blinked, wiping his sweaty brow on a dry shirtsleeve.

"Good," said Jack. "Now, we're gonna bank to the south and ride the current down the backside of this typhoon. You're gonna release lift gas from ballonets 1 and 2 at the same time." He watched his Egyptian protege blink and grit his teeth. This would be a steep learning curve. "Ready?"

"Well, no, not re—"

"You can do this, Asim."

"Captain—"

"Now," Jack ordered quietly. "Lean into the turn."

Asim gently pulled the control stick to the right, leaning over for leverage. He glanced at the gauges for the air bags and reached out toward the console with his left hand, flipping the switches for ballonets 1 and 2 to vent lift gas. He let the bags diminish about ten percent, then switched the toggles back to their neutral positions.

Stomachs leaped into throats as the ship nosed down from its original vantage, turning away from the whirling tropical wind, letting the maelstrom push them. The *Daedalus* dropped suddenly, and Jack had to grip the pilot's chair to keep upright. As the ship turned, he felt the spiraling currents nudge them down and around. They were about to get a big boost in speed.

"Here we go," he warned. "Everyone hang on!"

The *Daedalus* rode the outside of the storm like a toy car coasting down a spiral track. Halogen headlamps pierced the incessant rain, the whine of electric turbo-fans inaudible above the screaming wind. In the distance, a second pair of bright eyes shone through the darkness, turning to track with the ship in the lead.

The *Percival*, also lacking a dynamo but not having the benefit of Dhakiya's upgraded generator, struggled against the onslaught of wind and rain, Finally forced to open their course, they slipped further outside the arms of the storm.

Within minutes, the second set of lights disappeared into the stormy night sky, far behind.

The *Daedalus* surged ever forward in her wide, spiraling course. Her engines hummed at full power, useful only to keep the ship aimed in the right direction and avoid being pulled apart by the tempest. The envelope shuddered and shook, battered by the fury of the storm, each crew member swallowing in an attempt to equalize the air pressure in their inner ear as the ship careened through the night sky on a downward course.

Jack gripped the corner of the pilot's chair as he heard the first exterior cable snap, and the thought suddenly occurred to him that hugging the outer wind current of a typhoon for a speed boost might not have been his best idea ever.

⪻

By the time the storm moved inland from the Burma coast to blow itself out, dawn was threatening to shatter the sparkling purple veil of night over the Gulf of Siam. The *Daedalus* banked, low and lazy in the sky, starboard rudder cables dangling uselessly from the stern envelope. She came in from an almost southerly position over the Gulf, vulcanized metal skin shimmering in the early light like some kind of enormous, hovering fish.

If Bangkok ever slept, the casual observer would never know it. The sun had barely winked above the horizon and already the locals were swarming the streets, repairing the storm damage while *Monthon* officials surveyed losses. Before breakfast, the city was mostly back to normal function, and the *Daedalus* had secured permission to tie down at Don Mueang Airport, the oldest continuously-functioning airfield in all of Asia. Originally built for the Royal Thai Air Force, the facility had been servicing international commercial traffic for the past three years, increasing capacity each year. As a local ground crew mustered to help with the landing, a Fokker F.7 passenger plane bearing the KLM Royal Dutch Airlines paint scheme rose into the sky on a southeast heading.

A small, balding Thai of some fifty years was waiting at the debarkation point. He wore a simple white suit of homespun cloth, ideal for the humidity of mid-summer. A polished boar's tusk hung from a leather strap around his neck. Jack immediately recognized him from his entry in the 1927 *AEGIS Field Manual*. He jumped from the main gondola door, followed by Doc and Deadeye.

"Klahan Palaw?" Jack extended his hand, and the small man shook it.

Doc stifled a giggle. Like Mutt and Jeff, the two were almost comically mismatched in size.

"Captain Stratosphere!" he exclaimed in a reedy timbre, pumping Jack's arm enthusiastically. "You are the first agents to contact our field office! We are honored by your visit!"

Jack split his attention between addressing the bureau chief and giving orders to the crew. "Good to be out of that storm. Deadeye, you stay here and keep an eye on the goings-on. Tell Cipher to stay on the radio in case the *Percival* calls in. Say, Mr. Palaw, our sister ship was separated from us during the storm. We'll need additional tie-down space. Oh, and

Deadeye—tell Sparks to see to the rudder cables. You and Asim give her a hand if she needs it."

As Deadeye offered a quick two-fingered scout salute and returned to the ship, Doc offered her hand as well. Mr. Palaw, head still whirling from the avalanche of English spilling from the mouth of the American pilot, swapped Jack's hand for hers.

"Dr. Dorothy Starr, ship's medical officer," Jack explained, "and occult expert."

"Ah! Dr. Starr!" Palaw greeted. "You are most welcome!" Though heavily accented, his English was quite good, free of many typical inflections of the pidgin dialect so commonly spoken among the colonized people of Southeast Asia. But Siam had not been colonized. In fact, though politically and economically influenced by Great Britain, Siam was the only Asian nation to have remained free of European conquest.

Jack fidgeted anxiously in place, partly due to worry about Rivets, partly from having spent all night in a near-constant state of tension from the rough ride. "What's the latest, Mr. Palaw? Any word on the carriers? What intel do you have for us?"

Palaw understood the captain's anxiety, but was nonetheless disappointed to find them in a hurry. "Yes, yes. You understand I do not travel with such things," he explained. "All intelligence is stored at the office. You are welcome to examine everything there." His broad smile returned. "Come! The car is near-by."

Jack and Doc exchanged a look and shrugged. Apparently Bangkok had a an *actual* AEGIS field office, and not just a contact with some resources, as they'd encountered in Athens.

"Very well, Mr. Palaw," Doc nodded. "Lead on."

They piled into a black 1922 Model T touring taxi with the top down. Palaw slid to the steering wheel on the right, cranking the key in the ignition. The four-cylinder engine sputtered to life, reminding Jack how relatively quiet the giant thrusters on the *Daedalus* actually were in comparison.

Palaw knew Bangkok with native expertise. Jack and Doc were treated to a leisurely tour of the city, including side streets and narrow alleys barely wide enough to fit through. Although the influence of Western politics and religion could be seen in the occasional dress suit or Anglo figure, the streets of Bangkok were largely filled with earnest Thai faces. Jack kept checking his watch, fretting the entire way.

They arrived at a small ground-floor commercial space with a vacant receptionist station and an office in the rear. *Royal Stenographers, Ltd.* was stenciled on a plate glass window, which had evidently survived the previous night's storm due to its sheltered location within the city center.

They entered the vacant office, and Palaw locked the front door behind them. "My secretary will arrive later this morning," he said. "In the meantime, let us discuss your current status in here."

Palaw's office consisted of a twelve-by-twelve-foot room, furnished with a rattan desk, fan-back chair, and cushioned loveseat. A small lamp sat on the desk, switched off as the morning sunlight was sufficient to illuminate the office interior. A black candlestick telephone sat next to the lamp, and a framed *Nang Talung* shadow-puppet hung on the wall behind the chair.

Jack's attention was drawn to a device of brass gears and keys which sat atop a small corner table, under a glass dome similar to the cylinders that covered the dynamo generators on the *Daedalus*. He'd seen one before, in Edison's office. "Is that a stock ticker?" he asked Palaw.

"Ah," the small Thai man answered. "It used to be, but we use it to receive communiques directly, rather than having to rely on a telegraph office."

Doc noticed the art piece as she and Jack sat on the loveseat, and Palaw slid into the fan-back chair behind the desk. "Beautiful craftsmanship," she nodded.

Palaw turned to acknowledge the flat leather puppet on the wall. There was literally nothing else she could have been talking about: He flashed a gracious smile at Doc. "Thank you, Doctor. My father was one of the *Nai Nang*, a traditional puppeteer. This is the last one he ever created. It is Lord Brahma."

"I could tell, by his four faces," Doc smiled back, causing Palaw to arch an eyebrow in appreciation.

Jack was antsy, shifting nervously in the seat next to Doc. "What's the scoop, Mr. Palaw?"

Palaw unlocked his desk drawer and pulled a small handful of telegrams from within. "We've been monitoring all wireless communications. There has been much Silver Star activity in the region recently. Reports of slave trafficking in Burma...also the destruction of some sort of mineral refinery in Shanghai by a lone AEGIS field agent." He passed the pile of papers to Jack. "Last sighting of your super-carrier Zeppelins was two days ago."

"Drat," Jack muttered under his breath, sorting through coded telegrams and notebook pages.

Doc leaned close, peering over his arm at the various communiques. "Oh, Jack," she sighed. "You know as well as I that they could be just about anywhere."

Jack stood and nervously paced the small room. "I know," he said. "I'm just itching to find them. Worried about Rivets." Then he remembered their sister ship and her crew. "Worried about Duke and the *Percival*."

The ticker in the corner suddenly erupted in a series of staccato clicks, spitting out a thin strip of paper from a flat opening on the side. Palaw stood and went to retrieve the paper, waiting until the message was complete before delicately ripping it from the machine. Sitting back at his desk, he produced a small metal disc from the top drawer. Jack and Doc recognized it as a reverse-Caesar cipher wheel. The same kind they used to decrypt incoming communications, although since Marissa Singh had become their comms officer, they'd rarely seen a physical disc being used, as she carried the Caesar code and many variants in her head.

Palaw twisted the inner disc to line up a specific key. As Jack and Doc watched, he spread the long ticker tape out across his desk, opened a notebook, and began to scribble as he glanced from the tape to the disc and back. He was clearly used to this type of work, and had deciphered the message in less than two minutes. "It's from my contact at Don Mueang. The *Percival* has made contact with the airport," he announced. "They are just over an hour out."

"What's their status?" Jack inquired, handing the stack of telegrams back to Palaw.

The Thai man replaced them in the drawer along with the new message and its translated notebook entry. "Unknown. It says the commander wants an immediate conference with you."

Jack and Doc exchanged a knowing look.

"Duke knows we'd be meeting as soon as they got in," said Doc. "Standard procedure."

Jack nodded. "I wonder what's got him riled enough to make a specific request."

"We won't know if we stay here," Doc said, arching an eyebrow at the tall pilot.

Jack chuckled. "Indeed not. Mr. Palaw—"

But Palaw was already standing. "Of course, my friends. I'll return you to the airport right away."

They followed their contact back out to the black taxi parked at the curb. As Palaw locked the office behind them, Jack surveyed the narrow, stone-cobbled thoroughfare. An old woman in an open third-story window pinned her washing to a line above the adjacent alley. A thin man with no teeth and a floppy-brimmed hat negotiated a cart full of fish onto the road next to them. Locals ambled to and fro, carrying food, or lumber and various tools for city repairs.

It all looked very normal. A bit too normal.

Every hair on the back of Jack's neck stood at attention. He wasn't sure if it was Palaw's readily agreeable nature, or the subdued normalcy that permeated Bangkok's old town on this sunny, humid morning. It might have been the stark difference between flying through a tropical storm for hours and the quiet stillness in the absence of the typhoon.

When Jack silently nodded to the front passenger seat, Doc slid in without question. Palaw got into the driver's side and revved the engine to life. Jack climbed into the back and immediately checked both of his pistols for fresh magazines.

As Palaw put the taxi in gear and pulled out into the road, Jack saw the motorcycles behind them.

"Hey, honey?" he quipped, slipping one pistol back into its holster and readying the other, thumbing the safety off. "We've got company."

- CHAPTER 9 -

Palaw had left the top down, which was just fine by Jack. As the first motorcycle, a Czech-made Böhmerland cruiser, roared up behind them, he could see the rider was of a taller stature than the local Thai, and pale complected. Goggles hid the man's eyes, but his auburn hair was short-cropped and slicked back with pomade. He was dressed in a Manchu-style jacket of green and brown, and green *sado* trousers. Although not clad in the usual gray or black Astrum Argentum fatigues favored by Crowley's paramilitary soldiers, the man wore the telltale jackboots, and brandished a 9mm Luger over the handlebars.

Behind the first, at least two other motorcycles revved to catch up.

Palaw glanced in his side mirror and swerved hard to the left. That maneuver had the unfortunate result of putting his back in the gunman's line of sight. The soldier on the motorcycle fired, and Palaw's left shoulder collapsed suddenly, plastering the windscreen with spattered blood. He slumped forward on the wheel, cursing, and the taxi began to swerve and slow.

Doc blinked the initial shock from her eyes and, by instinct, pulled the wounded man toward her onto the passenger side of the bench seat. Palaw groaned in agony, clutching at his shoulder.

Lunging across his body, Doc grabbed the steering wheel and hauled herself into the driver's seat.

Jack popped up from the back, preparing to distract the motorcycle gunman, and shoot at him if possible. The Silver Star agent fired a second and third shot, both of which whizzed by Jack close enough for him to feel their wake. Jack planted one foot on the back seat and braced the other on the car boot, his right arm coming down to take aim with the .45.

Doc down-shifted and stomped on the accelerator, and the taxi lurched forward.

For the second time in as many months, Jack found himself launched from his vehicle of origin onto the one driven by someone who wanted to kill him. He landed astride the front fork of the motorcycle, clutching the handlebars with his left hand, his backside high enough on the fender to avoid contact with the tire. He grunted on impact, clenching his teeth. The momentary pain between his legs made him lose his grip on the Colt, which clattered away into the street, as his boot heels dragged the pavement on either side of the machine. The soldier opposite him seemed as surprised as Jack—at least momentarily. But then he pointed the Luger at Jack's chest and grinned with sinister intent.

Jack's meaty fist rocketed out of nowhere, pounding the gunman squarely in the nose. The agent's face flushed red and blood gushed from his broken appendage. The Luger fell away into the street.

Grasping the handlebars with both hands, Jack squeezed the brakes and ducked as low as possible, sending the rider over the front, somersaulting over Jack himself and onto the road. The sound of a neck breaking was audible over the screech of motorcycle brakes and flailing extremities. Almost immediately, the agent's body began to sizzle and smolder, sending tendrils of black smoke into the air.

As Jack hopped off the front fork to leap into the saddle, the other two motorcycles screamed past, intent on the taxi.

Now comfortably at the controls and facing the right way on the machine, Jack wheeled around in a wide circle, backtracking to the spot where he'd dropped his gun several blocks previous. There, on the cobbled street, the nickel plating of the Colt gleamed in the morning sunlight. He scooped it up and completed the circle, heading back toward the taxi once again. With his right hand opening the throttle and his left holstering the rescued .45, he sped to close the distance.

Doc swerved the taxi in an evasive fishtail pattern down the street, avoiding the merchant carts and pedestrians as though she were back on the obstacle course during her supplementary AEGIS field training. She heard a shot whizz past her head, then another. Glancing to her right, she could see the second motorcycle pull into range. Even armed with her revolver, the motorcycle was in her blind spot, making defensive fire inaccurate at best. And Jack was somewhere back there. She couldn't risk hitting him.

Splitting her gaze between the road in front of her and the driver's side mirror, she watched as the motorcycle gradually overtook them. She saw the second motorcycle pull into formation behind and to its right.

Suddenly the second motorcycle made a hard left, the driver's leg kicking out against the first vehicle's rear wheel. The momentary instability was all it took, and the first motorcycle wobbled and fell sideways in a violent crash.

Doc watched as the second motorcycle accelerated to match the taxi's speed, and rejoiced to see Jack salute her from the saddle. He flashed two fingers at Doc, then one.

Two down, one to go.

Doc smiled and swerved toward the road that would take them to the airport. "How you doing, Mr. Palaw?" she asked the groaning man in the passenger seat.

"Does this happen often?" he muttered weakly.

"More often than we'd like, honestly."

Jack slowed and pulled behind a wooden mule cart filled with produce. He didn't have long to wait before the final motorcycle zoomed past him, following the taxi. He revved the throttle and screamed out of the small crowd of locals and smoke from the street grills and cook fires.

Doc was still proving a difficult target, weaving across the road like a drunken race car driver. Jack reached under his arm and pulled his Colt from its holster, keenly aware that, between the multitude of civilians on the street and Doc and Palaw in the taxi, he'd need to check his fire extremely carefully.

The agent on the third motorcycle was following the same tactic as the last—cruising just out of sight in Doc's blind spot, firing at her from behind.

She glanced at the side mirror and saw Jack pull up fast. He squeezed between the taxi and the third bike, leaping from the saddle to the taxi's running board. The force of his jump pushed the motorcycle directly into the path of the third agent. Perhaps more aware than the others, the agent braked hard and swerved, missing Jack's motorcycle as it tumbled and rolled into the street behind them. Jack had made the error of consolidating targets, and the agent would make sure he paid for that mistake.

As the man throttled toward the taxi, Jack turned, gripping the car door with his right hand. The Colt whipped around in his left hand and a single shot rang out.

The agent's head snapped back and he fell limp, backward against the saddle. In the next moment, the bike slipped to the side and flipped laterally before skidding to a wrecked stop in the center of the road. Smoke billowed from the motorcycle's engine as well as its rapidly-desiccating driver.

Jack surfed the running board, still clutching the car door and scanning the distance for any more assailants. None appeared.

"I think we're clear," he announced over the growl of the taxi's engine.

Doc nodded at the wounded man to her left. "*We* might be, but I need to see to *him!*"

Jack vaulted the door into the back and looked over the front seat at Palaw. The man had already passed out, dark crimson blood staining his previously white, homespun shirt. "This is ridiculous!" Jack shouted, "Every port of call! Every damned one!"

Doc let a grim chuckle escape her lips as she drove on. "You say that like you're surprised or something!"

ℤ

The *Percival* came in just before noon, limping on a single thrust engine. As she descended over Don Mueang, Deadeye and Asim joined the local ground grew to assist with the tie-down adjacent to the *Daedalus*. The new arrival looked battered to hell and back, several cables and the dorsal guy-wire having snapped, and now dangling from the envelope.

"Looks a sight, *rafiq*," muttered Asim as he criss-crossed his anchor cable to the cleat embedded in the concrete.

Deadeye squinted at the stern rudder waving lazily in the breeze. "No kidding."

With the airship winched down securely, the side door popped open and slid astern on a scissor-hinge. Duke was first to the tarmac, followed by two of his crew.

"Ahoy there, Deadeye!" Duke bellowed as he crossed the hot cement toward his former crewmate.

Charlie met him halfway, and Asim approached from his flank, eager to hear Duke's tale.

"Cap's in the radio office in the terminal here," Deadeye explained, pointing at the large building a hundred yards to the west. "Checking in with HQ. Doc's at the hospital, working on our contact, Palaw."

"Heavens," Duke gasped. "What happened?"

"Silver Star agents, motorcycles, gunfire," Deadeye answered. "You know, the usual."

"How's the *Daedalus*?" Duke queried, appraising his sister ship's exterior.

Deadeye cocked a half-smile. "We looked almost as bad as the *Percival* when we got in, but Sparks has been hard at work in the engine room, and the rest of us repaired her outer envelope and cables. We'll be good to go in an hour. What about you all?"

"I'm sorry... Sparks?" Duke squinted.

"Cap gave her the name. She rigged up a new version of the engine dynamo that never needs winding. Output's ten percent better, too."

Jack ambled from the terminal's radio building as Deadeye explained. Duke saw him and saluted out of old habit.

"Captain," he addressed.

Jack returned the gesture. "What's your status, Duke?"

"As you can see," Duke began, gesturing toward the partially-deflated envelope and dangling cables, "we had a rough time of it. Lateral control linkages are either fouled or snapped. Starboard thruster is out of commission." He hesitated a moment, then added surgically, "And if I may, Captain—you're not in your S.E.5, shooting down German pilots over the Western Front. Single-fighter tactics don't apply when commanding two airships and their crews."

Jack wasn't surprised by the criticism; in fact, he'd been expecting much worse. The way in which he'd handled the previous night was weighing on his mind. He nodded, appraising the *Percival*'s sorry state from under his right hand, shielding his eyes from the noonday sun. "Agreed. I'm sorry, Duke. I shouldn't have tried to ride the storm like that. How much time to do you need for repairs?"

"At least twenty-four hours, I should think," Duke mused, satisfied with Jack's apology. "Less, if you can spare some hands."

Jack threw a glance at Deadeye, who anticipated the question.

"We should be done in an hour, be able to throw in on the *Percival*."

Duke scanned the airport grounds. The facility wasn't as primitive as many locales he'd explored with Jack McGraw, but something felt a bit...off. "I say, Jack, just how tenable is the situation here?"

Jack sighed. "Not great, to be honest. The field bureau here consists of the chief and his secretary, and the chief was shot by Silver Star agents while transporting us back to the airport. That means there's nobody in his office save for the secretary while Doc's pulling the bullet out of his shoulder. The agents knew we were in the city and where to come after us, which means they're monitoring all the radio frequencies and probably have the phone lines tapped. Cipher thinks she heard chatter over the Andaman Sea that led her to believe the Silver Star may have a base on one of the islands off the Burma coast. She also picked up a Morse signal in that same band. Said *DYNAMO KAPUT*."

"Bloody odd," Duke frowned, scratching his head under his officer's cap.

Asim squinted at the sky. "Maybe they couldn't get it to work?"

"Could mean anything, Asim," said Jack. "But no matter what, we can't waste any time rescuing Rivets. Now, I've checked in with headquarters and they're aware of our current status, and if we need to beat a hasty retreat, we've got more resources in Saigon and Hong Kong."

"Very good," said Duke. "What about Manila?"

"The Philippines?" Jack pondered. "Sure, why?"

Duke leaned in close, his tone conspiratorial. "Because the *HMS Covena* was attacked four days ago east of the Philippines. The cruiser *HMS Hawkins* rendered assistance and was also attacked. Just prior to their sinking, they reported two enormous airships in the vicinity."

"How'd you find this out?" Deadeye asked.

"We picked up part of a relayed report to the AEGIS field office in Delhi early this morning which included points gleaned from the initial SOS. It mentions Sir Reginald Yorke Tyrwhitt."

Jack scratched his head. "Should I know who that is?"

"He was my father's commanding officer on the *HMS Hart* back in '96. Our families have been friends for ages." Duke doffed his hat and nervously ran the band between his fingers. "If we can make contact with Sir Reginald, he might be able to give us a better idea of what the Silver Star are doing in that area, and where they may be headed."

Jack couldn't argue with a solid lead—the first real one they'd had on this journey. "How's your crew, Duke? Can you pull an all-nighter making repairs?"

Duke furrowed his brow in thought. "We're all exhausted, but if it means getting to a more secure location, we'll make the effort."

"That's the spirit," Jack nodded, clapping a hand on Duke's shoulder. He looked at Deadeye. "As soon as repairs on the *Daedalus* are finished, everyone over to the *Percival* to help get her sky-worthy."

"Aye, Cap," Deadeye nodded, gesturing to Asim and breaking away from the group, leaving Jack and Duke alone on the tarmac under the sweltering Siamese sun.

"Sorry to be a bother, old boy," Duke squinted. "I tend to be a nervous mother hen in the field."

"Not at all," Jack argued. "That's what we pilots call 'situational awareness'." Out of habit, he reached into his chest pocket for his pack of gum and remembered they hadn't found any to replace his Black Jack. "Anyway, if we're not secure here, and what you say about the sinking of the *Covena* is true, we haven't a moment to lose."

- CHAPTER 10 -

Both airship crews worked in rotating shifts throughout the sultry heat of the afternoon, and into the dark tropical night. Cables were replaced, aluminum struts were welded, envelope breaches repaired. Jack supervised from the main saloon of the *Daedalus*, with the side doors and all possible windows open for air flow. When the *Percival*'s starboard thruster was re-mounted, he operated the field crane personally. After Doc and Asim had finished plotting their next leg, Jack drafted them both into helping him make sandwiches for the ships' crews by creating a military-style KP assembly line in the galley.

Cipher picked up a Royal Army wireless transmission that had something to do with the disappearance of a certain Major Edwards in transit from Mombasa to Nairobi. Apparently he'd never arrived at the stockade, and his whole security detail was missing as well. The report hinted at possible native abduction, but Jack reasoned that either he was halfway to the nearest Silver Star training base by now, or Bwana Kifo had eliminated him. As much as the latter outcome would be a usurpation of justice, Jack couldn't argue that it was preferable to turning him into a pawn for Crowley's insidious plans.

Duke took an hour away from repairs on the *Percival* to negotiate some aid for Mr. Palaw and the AEGIS field office from the British consulate. By the time he'd finished hobnobbing with the ambassador and his staff, there would be a security detail of Royal Marines stationed both at the hospital and at the office in Old Town. This would allow Palaw to recover from his wound and begin the task of recruitment from the local Siamese population.

Sparks showed Darius Mahmoud, the *Percival*'s chief engineer, how to augment the existing dynamos with her system of magnets. Even minus one generator—as both ships were—each of the remaining nine cranking out an extra ten percent power meant both power plants were almost back up to spec. Keeping non-essential electrical systems off-line during transport would give every precious kilowatt to the thrusters.

Deadeye took up residence atop the *Daedalus* envelope, head covered in a wide-brimmed canvas bush hat, keeping watch over their section of Don Mueang Airport with a pair of field binoculars and his Springfield sniper rifle. He felt quite at home overlooking his tribe, protecting them with fire and thunder, but through the steamy heat of the day, he saw only the flight of tropical birds and a few commercial aircraft taking off or landing. Even so, nothing disturbed his vigil. He knew that if both Jack and Duke had misgivings about security, the worry was well-founded.

His counterpart on the *Percival* was Lt. Kate Shakespeare, an Englishwoman who'd grown up in British-controlled Arabia. She'd learned to shoot under the guidance of her Army officer father, and survival in harsh environments by her Bedouin mother. Though "illegitimate" by both British and Arab social standards, Kate had grown up a scrapper, following her father from post to post, living on Army rations and local hospitality. When she was sixteen, she joined a cadre of Egyptian "salvage crew", a glorified term for what they actually were: tomb raiders who engaged in unsanctioned, unscientific digs throughout the Nile Valley, harvesting priceless historical artifacts for sale on the international black market. She'd done a stint in prison and had made her living as a desert guide until AEGIS enticed her to take part in their operation. At just thirty, she was already a veteran of hard living and adventure.

She reminded Deadeye of himself in that way. He liked that. He liked her.

They spent the afternoon, each on their own perch, holding vigil over the airships. Kate's choice of arms was a Lee-Enfield .303 bolt-action rifle with scope, which Deadeye could respect, even though it didn't match his own preference. The only time she put it down was when she slung it to go below for a break, which was to say infrequently.

Over the course of the day they sent Morse code messages via hand mirror, and Deadeye found Lt. Shakespeare to have a rather earthy sensibility.

"Favorite movie star?" came a question in flashing mirror signals.

Deadeye pondered a moment, then replied with his own mirror. "Fairbanks. You?"

"Keaton makes me laugh."

"Shame about Valentino," he signaled, referring to the actor's death the previous year.

"I know real sheiks. He never impressed me."

"You're a hard woman."

"Soft in the right places. Just don't like phonies."

There was a pause while Deadeye tried to compose a reply, but before he could, another flurry of flashes caught his eye: "That's why I like you."

Deadeye couldn't remember having blushed in years, yet here he was—cheeks flushing red, butterflies in his stomach, and at a loss for words, even the kind flashed on a mirror. He hoped the two airships traveled together for a long time.

The repairs on the *Percival* went faster than expected, and the crews began to clean up and secure for launch just after sunset.

At 8:37 p.m., Deadeye spotted five Silver Star motorcycle scout units come out of the orchards and shoot through the security gate outside the airport, leaving the murdered guards where they fell. "We've got incoming! Five cycles, sidecars and small-arms!" he hailed over the ship's intercom from the top hatch.

Jack thought maybe they'd come from Nakhon Pathom or points west. Beyond the verdant fields and village farms of Siam spread the jungles of Burma, a lawless wilderness well suited to providing a mobile base of operations for the Astrum Argentum. The cycles were British-built Douglas RAs with sidecars, their occupants armed with MP-18 sub-machine guns. The sweltering night air was suddenly abuzz with angry hornets of lead.

Cables were uncleated and thrust engines powered on. Crews scampered to their flight stations.

"Battle stations!" Jack called on the intercom. "Ready to cast off—*we are leaving!*"

Deadeye heard the orders and knew he was needed below. He closed and sealed the access door with the twist of a handle, making his way down the ladder to the main saloon, past the gantry that would have taken him to the top turret, his primary station for observation and air-to-air skirmishes. When it came to air-to-ground altercations however, the dorsal guns were completely ineffective, so he would take up a position firing from the gondola.

As running lamps blinked on, the tarmac was suddenly bathed in halogen light. Black-clad soldiers on olive drab motorcycles stood out like swarming flies against a curtain. As turbofans revved up and the two dirigibles rose into the night sky, shots rang out from each gondola door. Deadeye took aim with the Springfield, peering through the scope. *Crack!* One sidecar gunner slumped in his seat, gushing blood from his throat. Charlie pulled back the bolt, releasing the spent cartridge as a new one rose into place. He quickly slapped the bolt forward and down, scanning for the driver of the cycle. As he lined up to target the center of mass, a distant shot echoed across the landing strip, and the soldier's head snapped to the side, blood and brain matter erupting from his ear.

Deadeye smiled. *Mark down a confirmed kill for Lt. Shakespeare.*

Shots continued as the airships ascended, gradually pulling out of range of the assailants. Fire-linked Lewis guns in the nose turrets tore up concrete and motorcycles like Mexican *piñatas* at a festival. Only one machine escaped, speeding away into the darkness. The ships let it go, banking east over the outlying farms and villages of Siam.

Deadeye counted three gunners neutralized by his own hand, and a gunner and two cycle pilots killed by Lt. Shakespeare in the *Percival.* Unless he was mistaken, this represented Duke's new crew's first altercation with agents of the Silver Star.

Of course it wouldn't be their last. That was clearly too much to hope for in their line of work.

On the *Daedalus* bridge, Jack reminisced about earlier times, when the Silver Star would actually infiltrate local trade guilds and civil authorities in order to strike a blow for their ideology. Nowadays, they just sent squads of foot soldiers or elite assassins to engage their AEGIS adversaries. Their tactics now resembled those of an overt war rather than a calculated long game. Either they were getting desperate, or growing brazen. Jack felt it didn't make sense to send such a paltry force against two crews of veteran field agents. Why not simply observe their movements and report up the chain of command? As he pondered the impending waste of human life, he realized he'd answered his own question. Crowley was not a tactician in the military sense, and human life was cheap to him. He had thousands of followers stationed throughout the world, ready and willing to die at his whim, all for the chance at a sliver of power or glory.

So they would keep coming. Always and everywhere. If only to prod and provoke and test their weaknesses. And when the agents were killed or captured, their soul contract invoked, their very life force bled away back to Crowley, feeding his already considerable power.

Doc found him later, slouched over a cup of coffee in the main saloon. "Hey, handsome," she smiled, squeezing his shoulder in a way that immediately released every tension and negative emotion in his body. "Penny for your thoughts?"

"Aww hell," said Jack, which surprised Doc to her very core.

She rarely heard anything saltier than *gosh* and *golly* from the man, so when he did utter a profanity of any kind, she knew whatever was on his mind was significant. And this was the second time she'd heard such language from him today.

"I guess it's not gonna get any easier, is it?" he asked rhetorically, sipping from the steaming mug and setting it back down on the table.

Doc went to the coffee pot and poured herself a cup. "You mean this last attack? No, no it won't get any easier. Crowley has his back against the wall, and a cornered animal—especially a wounded one—is the most dangerous kind."

"It's just senseless," muttered Jack. "During the war, at least we knew our enemy believed in what they were fighting for."

"Did they, though?" Doc asked with a sad look. She took her coffee to the table and sat down opposite Jack, trying to make eye contact. "Honestly, how many were true believers, and how many were just doing what they were told, or were fighting for the sake of fighting... and killing?"

The confused look that passed for deep thought which crept across Jack's face told Doc she'd hit mental pay dirt.

"When you really think about it," Doc said, almost in a stage whisper as she leaned forward for effect, "there's very little difference between a soldier going over the top and a Silver Star operative trying to outgun a couple well-armed AEGIS airships. Same justifications, same notions of tribalism, same promises of personal power."

Jack gazed out the window over his mug of coffee. "It's all a damn mess."

Doc chuckled low in her throat. "No argument there." She raised her mug in a toast. "To damn messes...and to the damn heroes who clean them up."

Jack allowed himself a half smile that Doc found completely irresistible. He raised his mug in return, finally meeting her eyes across the table. "Damn heroes."

ଓ

The flotilla charted a course east-northeast, across the bulge of Siam. By midnight they'd cleared almost halfway across the dark expanse of French Indochina. Small pockets of yellow-orange incandescent light stood out against the black curtain of jungle and terraced farmland. With the cruising speed of both ships improved to one hundred miles per hour, 2 a.m. found them over the South China Sea.

At 4 a.m., just south of the Paracel Islands, Cipher was coming back on duty when she picked up an odd transmission. She listened for a moment until the signal faded, making a note of the frequency. Two hours later, the radio detector picked up what appeared to be a seagoing vessel moving at a relatively fast clip on a northeasterly heading. As the sun began to rise over the eastern horizon, Cipher narrowed the band and did another sweep. There were multiple commercial and military vessels in the vicinity, the latter of which moved at a steady clip in well-known sea lanes. The others varied speeds depending on their course. The craft Cipher was interested in was perhaps six hundred feet long, of a slender cylindrical shape, and making a solid thirty-five knots, which was fast even for the nimblest of naval cruisers.

"Captain," she hailed to Jack, who was also two hours into his duty shift in the pilot's chair.

He tilted his head. "What have you got, Cipher?"

She described the findings of the radio detector sweep, adding a speed calculation that made Jack's jaw drop.

"Did you say thirty-five knots?" he blinked.

"Yes sir," Cipher replied.

"Might be one of the new Lexington-class carriers. How fast is the *USS Saratoga*?"

Cipher reached toward a row of technical manuals at her station, flipping open a new guide to US Navy vessels. "Rated at thirty-two-point-two-five and she's hit upwards of thirty-five at sea. But this ship is shorter by more than two hundred feet. Definitely not a carrier."

Jack gazed out through the windscreen array, dumbfounded. "Can't be a submarine either. The *Lir* class is the fastest in the AEGIS arsenal, and it's only fifteen knots surface speed."

"And it's gone," Cipher announced.

Jack turned in his seat. "What?"

"The vessel I was tracking. It's gone." Cipher frowned and tried to widen the radio band.

Doc emerged through the bridge hatchway, arms laden with maps she'd been examining aft in the chart room. Overhearing Cipher, she went to the nav station and began laying them out on the console. "That's disturbing," she said offhandedly.

Cipher turned open to the bridge. "Ma'am?"

"Vehicles don't usually just disappear, as a matter of course."

Jack nodded over his shoulder, acknowledging her arrival. "Unless they've been magically cloaked," he said, referring to an incident in the Bahamas, when the first *Luftpanzer* vanished in a searing flash of light.

"And who has the ability to magically cloak a ship?" Doc asked rhetorically.

Cipher took the radio headset from her ears, pursing her lips in thought. "With all due respect, Captain, Ma'am, it may be a leap to assume this is magical in nature. We're currently over a large body of water, and our radio detector can't scan beneath the surface. The most likely scenario is that the vessel either sank or submerged. Given its speed when it vanished from my screen, I'd bet on the latter."

Jack and Doc fell silent, chastened for the moment.

"Fair enough," Jack admitted. "I still think a submarine is unlikely."

Doc nodded. "But you're absolutely right, Cipher. There's no reason to jump to conclusions before we have more information."

Jack knew in his heart Cipher was right. He just wanted to know what could possibly do thirty-five knots underwater.

By 10 a.m., they could almost make out the land form of Luzon, the largest of the Philippine Islands, stretching north-south across the horizon. Cipher radioed in to Camp Nichols, operated by the US Army Air Corps, and the ships were given permission to land at their airfield a few miles outside Manila.

Just after lunchtime, the urban sprawl of Manila erupted with activity beneath them, and they banked south toward the Pasay district. The airfield was a long, flat, sun-baked expanse of packed clay with a control tower at the north end. Beyond the administration complex was a grove of trees that partially covered a recreation facility, and four large hangars stretched to the south. Jack counted at least six MB-2 bombers and four fighter escorts parked on the tarmac, all part of the 2nd Observation Squadron, charged with aerial mapping much of this mysterious and unexplored region of the globe. Between the hangars and the park was an open, vacant area. The airships were directed to land there.

Within thirty minutes, the *Daedalus* and *Percival* were tied down and the crews were greeted by a large and astonished contingent of American airmen, *ooh*-ing and *aah*-ing over the impressive profiles of the twin dirigibles.

Duke asked to use a telephone, and the commanding officer obliged. He was a slender, dark-haired fellow named Commander Roy Bloom, whom the pilots and mechanics called "Commander Cowboy", from his pilot call sign during the Great War. Bloom showed Duke into his office and pointed him toward the phone on his desk, then joined Jack and the others in the officer's club to share a drink and swap stories from the war.

The club itself was an open building the approximate size of a school gymnasium, with military banners representing different local units and squadrons lining the walls. An assortment of rattan tables and chairs was scattered around the periphery, leaving the center available for dancing. An Edison Diamond phonograph console near the bar, and the GE radio cabinet next to it, made that possible.

To Jack's delight, the small canteen at the front of the club stocked American chewing gum of various kinds. He quickly bought out their entire supply of Black Jack and stowed it back on the ship. He'd just returned for another round of beer and war stories when

Duke found his way in from the CO's office and took him aside.

"Any luck getting a hold of Sir Reginald?" Jack asked as he parked his backside on the corner of the table, gripping a clear glass of lager in his left hand.

"Affirmative," Duke nodded. "He wants to see us. Says it may have to do with the strange radio readings Cipher picked up."

"I don't know Manila," Jack admitted. "So I'll leave it to you to organize."

"I'm going to meet Sir Reginald tonight for supper at his hotel restaurant. You and Doc should join us."

"Is this a jacket-and-tie affair?" Jack scowled.

"Heavens, yes," Duke sighed at his American disdain of proper dress. "He's a Royal Navy officer and a peer." He paused for a moment, thinking. Then he added, "But if we three wear our full uniforms, he ought to be *somewhat* impressed."

- CHAPTER 11 -

Neela crouched beneath the broad fronds of a split-leaf palm and watched the beach with furtive eyes of aquamarine. Her triangular ears tilted and swiveled, picking up strange voices, feline olfactory senses telling her these visitors were not like those who had visited in the past. Not like the Creator or his kind. Not like Prendick, whose legend was still sung among her people. Not even like the Kanak from the east side of the island. These people from the sky—and their machines—smelled completely alien to her.

As she watched silently from the hill, a group of perhaps a dozen men and women in gray fatigues set up a base camp on the middle peninsula between the two large inlets from the east. Running to and fro, they gathered firewood, set up tents, felled trees, and set anchors for the giant ships in the sky. Overhead, the angry growl of Sopwith seaplanes brought the ancient legends of dragons to mind. Neela didn't like them. They were loud and reeked of petrol.

A loud whirring sound followed. Neela watched what looked like a ship's boat—but made of metal, with twin rotors, one to a side—descend to land softly on the white sand. It carried another half dozen gray-clad soldiers, who disembarked to the beach, slinging their weapons. As quickly as the skiff had landed, it was airborne again, lifting into the air with a great *whoosh*!

Neela peered out of the shadows and spied one of the anchors, set firmly around the base of a coconut tree. She followed the cable upward to where it terminated a couple hundred feet over the ocean. The ship was massive, casting a great shadow across the beach head, all but completely blocking out the sun. She scanned the side of the ship for any distinguishing markings or writing. As the daughter of the Sayer of the Law, she was offered a higher education than the common inhabitants of Sanctuary. She knew her letters and numbers, and had even read some books, which had survived the calamitous fire of '96.

L-U-F, she read silently. *Luff. T-P-A-N. Lufty-pan. Z-E-R. Zerr.* The characters after that simply appeared to be two of the capital letter I, which she assigned *I-I*, and deduced the ship must read *Lufty-pan Zerr Aye Aye.*

She flexed her lower claws and felt the pads of her feline digits clutch the earth. These people would not stay on the beach. Nobody who came to Sanctuary ever stayed on the beach. And these were not the benign traders the Kanak were. Neela wiggled her whiskers under the palm leaves and backed away from the overlook, standing on two legs as she went. The jungle shadows absorbed her black fur. A beige homespun blouse was visible, but her dark brown leggings and crimson sash disappeared with the rest of her. Feral ears twitched and turned to catch every bit of sound carried on the wind from the beach, and pronounced fangs became visible as her tongue tested the air.

Neela pondered whether to stay until dark and raid the camp, or go tell her people. Instinct told her to run as fast as she could. But not like the Old Way, on all fours as her people used to. She was the third generation of something different altogether. *'What is the Law?'* her father would ask. *'Not to go on all fours,'* she would answer. *'That is the law. Are we not men?'*

Standing with her back against the trunk of the nearby coconut palm, she slid into the jungle shadows and disappeared.

☙

Manila was a tangle of electric, telephone, and telegraph wires, strung across rooftops and towering poles in a chaotic spider's web of innovation. Her unique hybrid culture was evident everywhere: from the mission-style buildings of Spanish construction to the older influences of Indian and Japanese art and design, and of course the more recent American hustle and bustle that resulted in lively streets full of streetcars, horse-drawn hacks, motorcars, well-dressed pedestrians, and delivery trucks full of goods for sale. From Plaza Goiti to Luna Street in the old walled city of the Intramuros, commerce hummed and thrived with a life of its own. And with a population hovering somewhere in the number of 300,000 people packed into thirteen square miles, it was no wonder.

Everywhere the wafting smells of local cuisine permeated scenes of life in a multicultural melting pot. American sailors sampled the bars on the waterfront and the prostitutes that posed and strutted on the sidewalk. The only thing about the city transitioning from day to night was that the sun went down and street lamps came on.

The change from a Spanish colony to an American one had occurred two and a half decades ago, and whereas the American rulers were at first unpopular, a serious program raising the standard of living for the majority of Filipinos had greatly reduced the hatred of the Yanks and their bureaucratic rule from half a world away. The island territory was diverse, with civil and business activities taking place in a multitude of languages, incorporating ancient tribal customs. American authorities were hesitant to insert themselves into the middle of such things. Installing an all-Filipino legislature, and improving education, hygiene, and agriculture was an investment that paid off in a sugar boom.

Aside from the commercial attraction, the Philippines were also a valuable strategic asset, being a friendly, full-service port and the gateway to both the South Pacific and East Asia. It wasn't always roses and champagne, but the social and political situation in Manila was more stable than those in Haiti and many parts of South America, at the very least.

Jack and Doc rarely got opportunities to dress up and go out on the town while on assignment, so Jack set aside his grumbling at having to wear his heavy cotton AEGIS dress uniform on a hot, tropical summer evening. Just a couple hours, he told himself, then he could shuck the jacket and roll up his shirt sleeves.

Despite their discomfort, the trio of Jack, Doc, and Duke in their snappy blue uniforms presented an impressive picture. Doc wore a red officer's beret, while the two ship commanders sported blue combination caps, peaked in front above a red band and black bill. The AEGIS device of the winged shield bisected by a down-thrust silver sword shone both from the headwear's front, and the patch on the left jacket shoulder. The right shoulder sported the crew patch for the individual ship of service: Jack and Doc with the winged hammer and gear of the *Daedalus*, and Duke with the *Percival*'s knight chess piece in black. Rank pips gleamed from the collar: three apiece for Doc and Duke, four for Jack, who had been grandfathered into AEGIS at his captain's rank from the war. An assortment of special training badges lined up in rows on the left chest: Duke's contribution to the Communications and Admin divisions; Doc's organization of the Academic and Occult curricula and commendations for Exploration and Medical Science; and Jack's Test Pilot, Field Pilot, Exploration, and Special Operations commendations. Each was an inverted triangle an inch in length and width, embroidered with the icon and color scheme appropriate to the division and training in question.

The airship crews were unanimously happy for a night off, with Barrett, Mahmoud, Fraser, and Farmingham joining Cipher, Sparks and Asim at a local bar. Deadeye, as usual, volunteered to stay first watch, as did Kate Shakespeare on the *Percival*. They spent their evening talking back and forth via coded messages on the signal lanterns.

The uniformed trio took a taxi to an upscale restaurant in the Ermita district south of the Pasig River. With its open-air floor plan, marble columns, and electric ceiling fans whirring above, it was as opulent as one could find in the region. The place was packed. Tourists and wealthy Filipinos laughed and smoked imported cigars, drinking Italian wine. Local waiters in starched white livery brought endless courses of ethnic dishes combined with European influences. The strains of a live dance band filtered out from the adjacent ballroom.

They found their quarry at a table near the open courtyard, enjoying the offshore breeze and a gin and tonic. Vice-Admiral Sir Reginald Yorke Tyrwhitt was a tall, lean statue of a man, with angular features, a hawk nose, and close-cropped dark hair. His thin lips formed a straight line across his weather-worn face. He was by all accounts an attractive man for his fifty-seven years, with intelligent, discerning hazel eyes that peered out from under thick brows. He wore the uniform of a British Navy officer, his cap missing, no doubt checked with the restaurant staff.

When he saw Duke, the line of his mouth grew wider, but otherwise gave no change of expression. "Edward, my boy!" he hailed in a posh accent, standing from his wicker chair as the trio approached.

"Sir Reginald," Duke smiled as he overcame the instinct to salute. Instead he doffed his cap and offered a strong handshake. "These are my associates, Captain Jack McGraw and Doctor Dorothy Starr."

"Ah, yes," Sir Reginald said, shaking hands with each of them. "Your reputations precede you." He gestured at the chairs around the table, and they sat.

A waiter with slicked hair and a pencil-thin mustache arrived for a drink order. A Sidecar for Duke, Hanky Panky for Doc, and scotch on the rocks for Jack. The waiter smiled and disappeared, and Sir Reginald began the conversation, surprisingly, with small talk.

After some chat about the Great War and how everyone had spent the last decade, the waiter returned with the drinks, took their dinner order, and disappeared again.

"Good," said Sir Reginald, gazing across the table. "We shan't be interrupted again for some time."

"We understand your ship was attacked," Jack said bluntly, cutting right to the chase.

Reginald raised a bushy eyebrow in surprise. "Well, yes, in a manner of speaking...as you know, my job is Commander-in-Chief of China Station, British strategic command of East Asia and the Chinese coastal territories, having left my last ship command prior to the war. The past dozen years I'd been posted as a flag officer to a succession of flotilla and squadron commands. I'd only been overseeing China Station for a year, with the *Hawkins* as my flagship. On a routine run from Taipei to Shanghai, we picked up a distress call from the cargo ship *HMS Covina* about five hundred miles out in the Philippine Sea."

"Yes," Jack perked up. "Duke mentioned the *Covina*."

"Of course we went to assist," he explained. "Took fourteen hours at full speed to get there, and discovered the *Covina* had been completely scuttled, with most of her crew in the lifeboats. Just before dawn, about 0430, before we could so much as pull a single man aboard, something hit us amidships. Some sort of high-yield torpedo. Lookout picked it up and we executed some evasive maneuvers, but it had some sort of independent guidance."

Jack and Doc exchanged a glance. Was the Silver Star using radio-guided weaponry? And how did such a thing work while submerged?

"Heavens!" exclaimed Duke. "What did you do?"

"All we could do, considering our attacker was impossible to locate." Sir Reginald sipped at his gin and tonic. "We scrambled to the lifeboats and abandoned ship." He leaned forward, emphasizing his point. "It only took them one hit. They knew exactly where the magazine was. Next thing we knew, we were a few hundred sailors in rowboats on the high seas."

Doc squinted. "Didn't they come back to try to finish you?"

Sir Reginald shook his head. "That was the extraordinary thing. We lost a total of six crew in the explosion, but everyone else survived. The *Covina* lost four. Whoever it was allowed us to escape with our lives."

"That doesn't sound like the Silver Star," Jack muttered. Doc nodded in agreement.

"I say, what's this Silver Star?" Sir Reginald asked.

"It's an international organization," Doc explained, "run by an Englishman named Aleister Crowley. They operate worldwide, with spies and acolytes everywhere."

"Acolytes?" Sir Reginald queried. "What kind of organization is it?"

"It's an organization of the *occult* variety," Doc warned. "With a very well-stocked paramilitary arm."

"That's why AEGIS is involved," Jack explained. "We take the battle to them whenever we can, keep them from expanding their sphere of influence."

Duke looked uncomfortable spilling too much. "Nevertheless, this attack sounds decidedly unlike their *modus operandi*."

"Indeed," Sir Reginald nodded, slamming the remainder of his cocktail back in a single gulp. "But Eddie here says you're tracking a couple of unusually large airships, yes?"

Jack's eyes widened. "Yes, did you see anything?"

Sir Reginald leaned back in his chair, closing his eyes as the breeze wafted through. "Just prior to the torpedo attack, our radio operator picked up two large aircraft in the vicinity, on an southeasterly heading."

"Really?" Doc exclaimed, "Are you sure?"

"Completely," said Sir Reginald. "And the submarine that attacked us then turned and followed the airships to the southeast."

Duke glanced at his friends. "Now that's bloody strange."

Sir Reginald caught the eye of the waiter and signaled for another gin and tonic. "Bloody strange indeed."

Doc had a sudden thought. "Sir Reginald, we know the *Hawkins* was a warship—"

"Heavy cruiser, yes."

"But out of curiosity, what was *Covina's* cargo?"

The otherwise innocent question hung in the air between them, and Sir Reginald suddenly found himself uncomfortable. "I...er, that is...confidential."

Jack and Doc exchanged a knowing look.

"It was weapons," Jack blurted. "She was running guns in support of the nationalist government against the communists in Nanchang."

Sir Reginald's cheeks began to flush red, but he maintained his officer's composure. "I say, Captain. That's quite enough."

Duke winced at the prospect of his beloved Britain meddling in yet another civil war.

Jack, on the other hand, was unmoved. "Don't worry, Sir Reginald," he said, recalling similar exploits in Italy prior to his being drafted into AEGIS. "Your secret is safe with us. I just find it interesting that this submarine happened to target a warship and an arms transport, leaving the survivors alone."

Doc leaned forward, her fingers tracing the rim of her cocktail glass. "Agreed. We usually have a nose for Silver Star activities, and this doesn't seem like them at all."

"The two large aircraft, however..." Duke added.

Sir Reginald's face became a mask of marble. "Yes, well. I said I would talk to Eddie as a courtesy, given our family connection. But as far as I know, none of you are active military, and certainly not British military."

Duke sat back in his chair, tapping an index finger on the corner of the table. That comment stung a bit.

"Regardless of the attacker's motives," Sir Reginald continued, "the submarine engaged in an unprovoked act of aggression, and I intend to hunt it down and sink it."

Doc's lips pursed into a shape that meant some razor-edged snark was imminent. "One could argue that the presence of an arms transport and a heavy cruiser in the region is provocation enough for action."

No one would have believed it were possible for Sir Reginald's face to become even tighter and more stoic, but it happened. He reached for his pipe and proceeded to fill it with a pinch of loose tobacco from a pull-string pouch next to the ashtray. He said nothing, and a cold pall settled about the table.

Duke felt a personal need to salvage the meeting. "Sir Reginald," he said softly, "give us a week to see if we can't track down the sub and find out more about who is operating it and what their motivations are. Don't send in the Royal Navy just yet."

The vice-admiral leveled a practical gaze at Duke, biting down on the stem of the pipe and striking a match to light the bowl. "I've booked passage on an American transport to Taipei on Wednesday, at which time I shall have to file my report with the Admiralty. I will then await further orders. You have until the arrival of those further orders to investigate to your heart's content."

"Fair enough," Duke said quietly. He looked at Jack, who tipped his glass to Sir Reginald and smiled.

"To your health, sir," said Jack.

- CHAPTER 12 -

Neela found her village as the sun was setting. It occupied a flat area on a ridge of the midmost of four dormant volcanoes which had created the island. The place lay a couple of miles east of the beach head, and was rich in natural defenses like craggy paths, poisonous plants, and sheer precipices, all of it tucked deep in the cover of the jungle and invisible from the sky.

Already the citizens had assembled, the elders sitting in conference in a line before the ring of bamboo and palm leaf huts. A series of six-foot-high bamboo torches illuminated the community of some two dozen individuals. Ranging in age from second to third generation, the human-beast hybrids dressed in a mixture of homemade clothing and castaway fashion, bits and pieces of Victorian technology and affectation. A pig-woman in tribal dress stood next to her mate, a half-bear in blue canvas trousers, as a pair of pre-adolescent simian twins stared agape at the proceedings.

"Are they not men?" one elder, an ox-human hybrid wondered aloud. "Like Prendick?"

A dog-faced woman with a gray muzzle nodded. "Should we not welcome them in friendship?"

An older panther-man in ornately woven robes folded his arms and frowned, whiskers testing the wind. He cracked a half-smile, knowing his daughter was nearby, though he could not see her beyond the ring of torches. "What if they are men like Prendick?" he asked the panel of elders and the gathered crowd. "What then?"

Neela stepped into the amber glow of the flickering torches and the crowd parted for her. She was known as an educated, articulate young woman, heir to the position of Sayer of the Law. "They *are* men," she announced. "They are many. And I do not think they come in peace."

"How do you know this?" asked the ox-man, pulling his loose tunic a bit closer against the chill evening breeze.

Neela strode to the center of the gathered beast folk, her wooden knife-weapon slung safely in the red sash around her waist. She bowed before the elders, acknowledging the Sayer of the Law. "Father," she nodded.

The panther-man leaned forward, advanced age evident in his slow, deliberate movements. Aquamarine eyes, the same as Neela's, gleamed and sparkled in the firelight. One corner of frosted-gray muzzle pulled up in a sort of half-smile. "Go ahead, my daughter. How do you know their intention?"

"They bring many soldiers, with guns," Neela answered. "Guns like Nemo's."

This sent a murmur through the crowd. The name of their protector was not often spoken aloud.

The dog-woman raised a furry hand. "But Nemo is good!"

Another murmur, this one of approval, swelled through the assembly.

"That Nemo is good," growled the Sayer of the Law, "does not make all men good." He nodded at his daughter in encouragement. "That the Kanak trade fairly does not mean these sky-men will trade fairly. What else?"

"They came in numbers, with sky-ships great and small, like a colonizing army." She looked directly at her father, referencing her education. "As in the histories taught to us by Dr. Nariaal."

At the mention of this name, the crowd grew quiet and respectful.

Neela paced in silence between the villagers and elders for a few moments, finally addressing the combined group. "We should ask the counsel of Dr. Nariaal. He will know whether the sky-men come in peace or in war."

"Dr. Nariaal continues his studies at the House of Pain," said the elder panther-man.

"Has he not reached out on the talking box?" Neela asked. "Have you not called for him?"

The ox-man elder folded his arms across a massive chest. "Dr. Nariaal is wise," he admitted, "but he does not rule Sanctuary."

Neela spun to face the elder, her face a mask of righteous indignation. "No one *rules* Sanctuary," she spat. "Dr. Nariaal is the wisest of us, which is why we need his counsel."

"Enough talk," the Sayer of the Law grumbled. "We will contact Dr. Nariaal on the talking box. After counsel, we will decide what to do."

With that, the assembly was over. The elders stood, returning to their huts while the villagers resumed their prior activities.

The Sayer of the Law beckoned toward the young panther-woman. "Neela, come with me."

She followed her father into his jungle hut. As a village elder and the Sayer of the Law, he was granted a bit more space, and access to technology the common citizens of Sanctuary were prohibited from using without specific permission or instruction. Although relatively spacious, the panther-man's lodge was simple and sparsely furnished: a bamboo bed, a rattan stool, and an old walnut desk—Victorian craftsmanship by the look of it, possibly an heirloom from the days of Moreau. On the desk was a worn wooden box, connected to a wire which ran up one of the upright wall posts and out into the rainforest. It had a mounted microphone and candlestick earpiece, with a brass hand crank on the right side.

They went to the desk, and the Sayer of the Law pulled the stool with him to sit on. As Neela watched, the panther-man ran a claw along the top of the wooden telephone housing.

The ape brothers from the village assembly poked their heads into the hut. "Sayer?" one of them asked softly, hesitation quavering in his voice.

The panther-man closed his eyes and smiled. "Come in, young ones. I am going to speak to your uncle."

Both youngsters entered, shoving each other as they moved to toward the desk.

"I told you he was going to call Uncle on the Talking Box."

"I can't wait until we can go with Uncle on his study journeys."

The Sayer of the Law had only to cast a sideways glance, and the ape-boys became silent and still.

Grasping the crank handle with a fur-covered right hand, he plucked the earpiece from its cradle with the other. He gave the crank a half dozen quick turns, and waited for the disembodied voice of Dr. Nariaal to greet his ear. There were a few seconds of static-rattled quiet, then:

"This is Nariaal," came a low, booming voice.

"This is the Sayer of the Law," the panther-man spoke into the mounted mouthpiece. "I call upon you for counsel in an urgent matter."

"I believe I know what you're referring to," the low voice said. "The incursion of men onto our island. I have seen their aeroplanes over the interior."

"Arrow...planes," the Sayer repeated, not grasping the concept of the word.

"Yes," Nariaal answered. "I fear these men are not like the Kanak. They are men, but they are not to be trusted, as they break the Law."

"Which Law?" asked the Sayer. "They walk on two legs..."

"Not to spill blood, and not to eat flesh."

Sayer's eyes widened in horror at the thought. "They spill blood...like the Maker?"

There was a long silence as the line crackled. Finally Nariaal answered. "You remember the tales you were told, of the House of Pain..."

"Yes."

"You remember the horrors of Moreau, as they were written..."

"Yes."

"Then listen to me, Sayer of the Law, and take heed. These men are worse than even the Maker, worse than all the horrors of Moreau combined. Gather your village and flee away from the coast where these men have come. Come to Fort Sanctuary, and receive the protection of our walls. Together we will develop a plan to rid ourselves of these invaders."

The Sayer of the Law paused, eyes shut and lost in thought. "Will you...will you summon the Water Soldiers?"

Static became the rumbling baritone once again. "I leave the House of Pain tomorrow to return home. But I will contact the Water Soldiers before I depart. Be swift, Sayer of the Law. Be safe."

The line went dead, and the Sayer of the Law sat on his low stool, telephone earpiece in hand, wondering how he would justify a complete evacuation of the hillside village.

CR

The crews of the *Daedalus* and *Percival* slept well at the airfield, rising at dawn for coffee and *silogs* of garlic fried rice and eggs at the officer's club. They bade farewell to Commander Cowboy and headed to their respective duty stations. By the time the sun had crept above the eastern horizon, both airships had powered up turbofans and gently lifted into the air.

Ascending to two thousand feet and weaving a braid-like pattern, the ships charted a course southwest, across the broken Luzon peninsula, past Samar Island, and out over the vast blue expanse of the Philippine Sea. From there, they skirted north of Palau, through the Caroline Islands. Every hour, the comms officer of each ship did a long-range radio scan of the vicinity. The plan was to keep Apia in Samoa as their next port of call, unless they picked up data that would lead them somewhere else. At full throttle and without a headwind, Apia would take them about fifty hours. In the meantime, Cipher and Farmingham wore their headsets, keeping vigilant for any news of ships being attacked in the region.

The seemingly endless blue beneath them was an adjustment for Jack. He'd only ever flown a few hours outside sight of land. In fact, most of his flight experience had been going between point A and point B on a map with place names and solid earth to land on or shoot at. Fortunately, both Doc and Cipher happened to be excellent navigators, and he trusted their calculations. And whereas an airplane or diesel-powered warship had a finite range, the LR-3 airships could run as long as their dynamos generated power to the turbofans. They needed only worry about provisions and potable water, the restocking of which was accounted for in their plotted itinerary.

At about 3 a.m., Farmingham at the *Percival*'s comm station picked up a distress call. The British submarine *M-2*, roughly 470 miles north-northeast of New Ireland, had been attacked by an unknown hostile vessel. The *M-2* had taken engine damage and was limping southwest, back to the nearest friendly port:

Kavieng. They'd launched their single Parnall Peto reconnaissance seaplane, which had sent the hostile packing, at least as well as they could figure. The *M-2*'s ASDIC hydrophone had tracked the hostile heading away to the south, toward the Solomon Islands. The Peto was only rated for two hours flight time between refueling, and it had already been aloft for twenty minutes, scanning the black ocean with its single searchlight.

Jack patched in through the *Daedalus* radio and instructed the *M-2* to keep their speed and course. They would arrive within the hour and render whatever assistance possible.

Doc sighed. "Well, I guess we're closing in on our mysterious submarine, if not the Silver Star supercarriers."

"Awful lot of British ships being targeted," Jack muttered. "I wonder what their beef is."

"Also," added Doc, "what's ASDIC?"

"Allied Submarine Detection Investigation Committee," answered Cipher. "The Admiralty has started outfitting all military craft with a special hydrophone which gives the crew a sort of echolocation, like a dolphin or whale."

"It's the underwater equivalent of our radio detector," Jack added.

Doc nodded, trying to convince herself that it wasn't nearly as funny-sounding as she thought, but was only partly successful at keeping an adolescent smirk from creeping across her face.

Just after 4 a.m., the two airships dropped down over the struggling *M-2*. Several members of the submarine crew were hoisting the Peto back aboard with the special crane that jutted out over a specific deck-mounted hangar, folding its wings as they slid it home. Upon seeing the two approaching airships, the British sailors began to hasten their activities. Two electric searchlights were produced on the deck, pointing upward and scanning the night sky.

The *Percival* dropped down to about thirty feet, illuminating the deck of the *M-2* with her halogen floods. While Sheila Barrett kept the ship steady, Duke lowered a tow cable from the center gondola hatch. The steel line, weighted by a nautical-grade hook, clattered to the deck of the submarine, and two sailors ran to hook it to a forward cleat. The *Percival*'s twin engines hummed as she thrust forward at half speed, *Daedalus* keeping a watch position above and behind both her sister ship and the submarine she towed.

After pulling the wounded sub for six hours, the *Percival* radioed the crew to unhook the cable. The sun was already high in the eastern sky and the Peto was refueled. They were only another hour or so out of New

Ireland—safe enough to allow the Peto to fly escort the rest of the way.

What the airship crews hadn't mentioned to the captain of the *M-2*, nor why they felt the sub would be safe on its final approach home, was that Cipher had picked up a message. And not just any random transmission, either. This message had been focused in a very narrow band, a frequency Cipher knew to be used by pirates and certain other lawless individuals.

It was in a standard reverse-Caesar code with the key set to D-N, in English, and it said simply: *'Daedalus and Percival, send word from Apia. Will contact.'*

- CHAPTER 13 -

When the black dragons came from the sky, the native Kanak people of the island's north shore surely thought the end of the world was at hand. Great, roaring machines swooped and dived over the village, spitting fire and death from their mouths, reducing the primitive dock to shattered flotsam in the water. Dugout canoes and outriggers were scuttled in the tiny natural harbor, as huts of bamboo and palm-thatch ignited under a hail of phosphorous ammunition. Chickens and pigs kept as livestock were torn to pieces in the onslaught. Those who by some miracle survived the first pass escaped into the thick jungle, leaving their paltry possessions in what used to be their home.

When at last the planes had ceased their murderous campaign and moved on over the island's interior, a metal skiff descended from above, whirring metal blades spinning within a hoop on each side. The machine landed on the beach beside the wrecked pier, and five soldiers in gray fatigues hopped down from the vehicle, submachine guns at the ready. The one in front waved the others forward, and they marched into the burning village together. Those who survived the planes would be taken prisoner by the soldiers. There were only two options: compliance or execution.

The gyro skiff rose into the air behind them, sending sand and burning palm embers whirling in a mad dance of death and destruction. When the soldiers had examined the vacant village and disappeared into the jungle after the survivors, all that was left was a smoldering beach fire where peaceful people had lived for generations.

☙

"Cipher says the transmission was on the so-called 'pirate band' she monitors," Jack explained. He and Doc stood over the desk in the aft chart room, looking over a large map of the Pacific islands. Jack marked an X on their current position—just east of Bouganville in the Solomon Islands—with a red wax pencil. He scrawled another *X* over Apia in the tiny chain of American Samoa.

"Fair enough," Doc said. "At this point we have no reason to believe it's a hoax."

"Whoever it is knew our ship registries." Jack took a large T-square and traced along its edge between the two *X* markings. "A little over a day at full speed," he deduced.

"Then what?" Doc asked.

Jack could tell she was exhausted. This had been a long mission. "Then what, *what?*" he shot back.

"What do we do when we arrive at Apia?" Doc asked, hands on hips. "Contact them again, get lured out into the middle of nowhere and murdered?"

"It's true," Jack said nervously. "There's not a lot out here. But it's our only lead on the supercarriers. I figure once we make contact again, the rest will sort itself out."

"Famous last words," chuckled Doc.

"Oh, I've got a ton of famous last words," Jack said. "'How hard can it be?', and 'I volunteer' chief among them." He traced an index finger along the wax line. "What's our provision status?"

Doc turned to a clipboard on the desk and flipped a few pages without picking it up.

"We're good for about five, maybe six days," she said. "If we hold back on showers to conserve water. Should be good to Apia, no problem."

"Lovely," Jack replied. "Twenty five hundred miles in an aluminum can that smells like dry-roasted peanuts."

Doc snaked her arm around Jack's waist as she moved toward the door. "Aww, it's not that bad," she smiled, kissing him on the cheek. "You have a decidedly non-peanutty musk."

"Good to know," Jack said, returning her affection.

"And licorice breath," she added, pulling away with a pat on the chest.

Jack laughed, realizing he was still working on a stick of Black Jack from two hours ago, and it was now a stale, rubbery glob. "Well that ain't gonna change any time soon, sister."

Doc opened the chart room door and winked at him as she stepped out. "Hmm. I may have to reconsider this entire relationship."

Jack began rolling the chart into a tube, calling after her. "Why can't you love me as I am?"

The *Daedalus* and *Percival* soared southeast on their course, occasionally banking to take advantage of the summer wind currents and avoid the squalls that came seemingly out of nowhere. They left the Solomon Islands on the western horizon, keeping Fiji and Tonga far to the south. The deep cerulean blue of the South Pacific spread out beneath them, shimmering silver in the morning and darkening to a deep cobalt as the sun traversed the equator and faded during the night. If not for the shifting of astronomical landmarks and modern instrumentation, they might not have thought they were moving at all, so vast was the expanse of blue hues above and below, delineated only by the horizon.

Jack and Doc usually tried to split their shifts to avoid a lot of overlap, when they would be off duty together; this was by design, to avoid any ill feelings from the other crew about their "fraternization". Ironically, everyone on the crew knew them to be a couple—with a child, no less—and trusted them implicitly. There were no ill feelings to begin with, nor would there be any.

Doc left the nav station on the bridge at just after 2200 hours, and found herself tapping at the door to Jack's stateroom instead of opening her own door across the main saloon.

"Come in," came a tired response, followed by an actual yawn.

The door popped open and swung inward, revealing the standard LR-3 stateroom in all its seven-by-twelve-foot glory: a bank of tempered windows canted outward at the top, and lacquered canvas walls covered perforated aluminum studs. A locking wardrobe/dresser unit sat against the external wall forward, while the bunk lay short-ways, perpendicular to the windows, against the aftermost wall. A small, square desk between the bed and locker also functioned as a night stand.

Jack sat up in his bunk, wearing only a pair of drawstring boxer shorts. Blinking tiredly, he switched on the bedside light. "Doc?" he mumbled, concerned. "What is it?"

"Want some company?" Doc smiled as she entered the small stateroom and shut the door behind her, locking it quietly.

When they returned to duty, Jack six hours later and Doc eight, they radiated contentment. Not a soul on the crew didn't know what had occurred in Jack's cabin, nor did they comment on it, but everyone wondered why it'd taken so long during the mission, especially given their loving family image away from AEGIS operations. Although they projected an air of professionalism and propriety in the field, the *Daedalus* crew knew how passionately they loved each other. It was not something that would raise an eyebrow. Not on board, at any rate. It had just never happened on a mission before now.

As Jack's watch hit noon, they came in low over Apia. The city was a casual sprawl of Polynesian-style grass huts and western timber homes which radiated outward from the harbor lagoon. A single hotel sat to the north side of the harbor, and a few brick government buildings formed landmarks for Jack and Duke to make their approach. *Treasure Island* author Robert Louis Stevenson had called the island home for the last five years of his life, writing of the gentle nature of the native people in his *A Footnote to History: Eight Years of Trouble in Samoa*. The territory had been under German and American rule prior to the Great War, and now existed under New Zealand administration, which was growing ever more unpopular. Even so, Apia was a relatively stable oasis in a literal ocean of uncertainty.

The two airships circled the island of Upolu, looking for a landing facility, but there was no actual landing strip to be found. They would have to circle back around to the harbor and tie down at the docks. They had just received the harbor master's permission to land, when Cipher broke in with sudden news.

She'd been sending a coded greeting on her "pirate band", and had picked up a direct reply from the mysterious party. Jack ordered both ships to station-keeping until the incoming transmission could be deciphered. Then he ordered, "All hands to bridge," over the intercom. Asim came forward from his quarters and took the helm, while Jack leaned over Cipher's chair, watching her scribble letters as the beeps came through her headset. Sparks and Deadeye stood on the other side, tense with excitement. Doc remained at the navigation console, charts at the ready.

Marissa Singh had the call sign of "Cipher" for a reason. Aside from fluency in multiple languages, she was an ace when it came to codes. Once the key came through, she could convert the Morse code signals into letters, which she then transposed along the reverse-Caesar wheel according to the key, writing the result in her official communications log. All of it done in her head, on the fly.

"Lincoln Island, three-four degrees five-seven minutes south, one-five-zero degrees three-zero minutes west. Do not stop. Will contact on arrival."

"Chart," Jack said, turning toward Doc and the nav station.

"Got it," she replied, walking a small tin compass across the map like a cowboy moseying to a gunfight. She marked the coordinates on the chart with her red wax pencil, turning the giant sheet of laminated paper to face Jack across the console. "It's about two thousand more miles out into nowhere."

Jack scowled. "What the devil...?"

"Oh, Lincoln Island is real," Doc assured him. "Supposedly. If we want to believe anecdotal evidence. Just south of Maria Theresa Reef. But it hasn't been officially surveyed, and keeps disappearing from more recent commercial maps and charts."

"Whoever this is," Jack sighed, "wants us to trust them to meet us two thousand miles out in the middle of the South Pacific, at an island which may or may not actually exist."

Doc nodded. "Talk about a long shot."

"Used to *them*," Deadeye winked at Doc from the comm station.

"Sparks?" Jack turned to look at the engineer standing next to Deadeye. "We've been pushing full speed for over twenty-four hours. How are the systems holding up?"

"We're at maximum output for what each dynamo circuit can handle, but we're also missing one per ship, so we're taxing the other nine a bit more than we would normally be doing." Her left hand dropped into the side pocket of her tool belt to fidget with a crescent wrench. "But so far, we haven't had any problems. I think we could push on another day."

"If Sparks is confident in the power systems," Cipher announced, "then I say we push on."

"Asim?" Jack patted the back of the pilot's chair.

"I promised you a hundred percent when I joined AEGIS," said the young pilot. "And I meant it."

Jack looked at Deadeye, who chuckled and slapped his shoulder.

"You know I'm along for the ride, Cap."

Jack turned back around to face Doc across the navigation desk. She immediately rolled her eyes with a barely-hidden smile.

"You know better than to ask *me*, Captain Stratosphere," she said quietly.

"The ayes have it," said Jack. "We push through another day. Everyone back to your stations. Cipher, answer 'affirmative' using the same code key. Relay new orders and course to the *Percival* crew. Let me know if Duke has any questions, I'll talk to him on the two-way radio." He clapped a hand on the side of the pilot's seat, getting Asim's attention. "Okay, mister, you're not back on duty for another couple hours. Go relax."

Asim nodded, unstrapping from the pilot harness and stepping out of the chair. "Call if you need me, *Naqeeb*."

As he left, Jack strapped into the seat once again, but suddenly aware that he'd never heard Asim call him by that name before. "Hey Cipher..." he began.

"*Naqeeb* is Arabic for 'captain'," came the reply as if she'd anticipated the question a split-second before it was asked.

"Say, that's not bad," Jack said as he mulled the nickname over in his head. He pulled a stick of gum from his pocket and unwrapped it from the waxed paper envelope, cramming it into his mouth. "*Naqeeb*..."

They filled their ballast tanks and water reserves, and in less than an hour, the sister ships had left Samoa, and anything resembling friendly civilization, behind to the northwest. Farther and ever farther into the vast blue expanse of the Pacific, passing areas rarely explored and never flown over. Twenty hours would have them at the mysterious coordinates by about 0900 the next morning. Unless something out of the ordinary happened.

Jack's heart sank and he winced almost audibly. He'd thought it. He'd tempted fate.

'Unless something out of the ordinary happens'? That's a good one, McGraw. Really just marvelous.

- CHAPTER 14 -

Maria Blutig paced the white sand beach, directing the construction of her ritual site. Soldiers scurried to and fro, dragging freshly-cut logs in work crews, sentries setting up elevated guard towers and a picket wall against the rainforest beyond. Already they'd clear-cut a huge swath of jungle back from the beach, claiming the real estate for their diabolical fortress.

She strode toward a slightly-built man in round glasses overseeing the unpacking of several wooden crates. He had a tinge of gray at the temples and mustache, but she remembered him from the early postwar days of the *Astrum Argentum*. "*Herr* Himmler," she barked. "Status report?"

Heinrich Himmler blinked those same sunken blue eyes behind the round frames of his spectacles. There were crows feet now, understandable in as much as he was currently serving two masters: Nazi party *Führer* Adolf Hitler in Berlin, and "Great Beast of Mankind" Aleister Crowley, allegedly back in Paris. Neither could know of his service to the other.

"The batteries are ready," Himmler reported. "One damaged in transport, but otherwise all accounted for. They will be ready when you are."

"*Sehr gut.*" Satisfied, Maria strode toward the ritual area.

The altar was taking shape. Made of coconut palm logs rafted together with sisal rope, there was to be a central chamber within which the mage—in this case Maria herself—would stand, directly underneath a flat focal area which would support the mechanical trap. At equal level to the central chamber and altar area there would be a raised holding cell, capable of containing up to four sacrificial victims, with a ladder down to ground level. Soldiers would herd sacrifices up into the holding cell, the spirit trap would be set, and Maria would open a portal to some unidentified nether realm, summoning the eldritch horror that lurked within. When the summoned creature came through and was distracted by feeding on the sacrifices, the trap would be deployed, the demon captured and used as a potentially limitless battery.

There were twenty crates, each containing ten traps. If they were successful in this venture, even anticipating a ten percent failure rate, they would come away with almost two hundred Infernal Machines. Useful indeed.

Himmler paused, trying to meet her eyes. "And, *Fraulein*, if you wish to speak—"

"Not here," she hissed. "Or now. I will summon you at the right time."

Himmler nodded and returned to his work on his inventory.

As Maria headed back to the landing zone where two gyro-skiffs were waiting at any given time, a detachment of scouts marched out of the jungle with eleven prisoners in tow. Seven were male, four female, all large and strapping Kanak people, the indigenous Melanesian inhabitants of New Caledonia. This place was far from their usual fishing grounds, but there was much the Silver Star did not know regarding the island or its inhabitants.

As Maria passed the prisoners, she nodded at the ranking scout, then at the stockade against the jungle wall. The scout thrust the stock of his MP-18 into the kidney of one of the male prisoners, pointing at the stockade. Maria continued to the first gyro-skiff and addressed the pilot. "Take me back to the ship," she ordered.

The pilot saluted, revving the twin rotors to life and ascending into the air.

It won't be long now, Maria thought. *Soon we will have the eldritch energy to power all sorts of new technology, with naught to stop us.* She squinted into the impossibly blue sky, a headache starting to take hold. *Now,* she thought. *Now, I need some time to meditate, to gather all of my strength.* She thought of Rivets, curled up in her brig. He'd shown great resistance to conditioning through torture. But if he would not convert to the service of the Astrum Argentum, he would at the very least provide some sacrificial energy in the summoning in just thirty-six hours time.

She closed her eyes and recalled the rush of power she'd received from almost having summoned Ammit, Soul-Eater, Devourer of the Dead, in the buried temple at Naqada. So much blood spilled into the earth, so many souls absorbed. She'd been so close. But she'd had to divert that energy from the summoning to make her escape.

Still, it was all practice—practice at greater rituals, with higher stakes.

Himmler's choice of Noble's Isle had been a stroke of genius. Plenty of raw materials to build their ritual facility, a ready supply of natives to sacrifice, and an isolated area in case the summoned entities were too strong to handle, requiring evacuation. Best of all, no local government to cause them delays. As far as anyone on Himmler's staff knew, Noble's Isle had been the home of a British surgeon and vivisectionist named Moreau, who was rumored to have performed all sorts of horrific medical experiments on the local animal population in an effort to elevate their intellect and sentience. Allegedly the beast folk had rebelled, and Moreau's entire compound was burned to the ground, the only witness having returned to England in 1896 and retired to a small estate in the rural countryside.

Maria smiled to herself. There was already so much pain here—the island was steeped in it. She could use that pain when it came time, to lure the demons as one would set a snare trap for a rabbit.

The skiff came to a soft landing on the flat dorsal runway of the *Luftpanzer II*, and Maria stepped out, allowing another small work party to enter the rotor craft. It promptly lifted off again, ferrying the soldiers down to the beach head. She gazed out over the dorsal surface of the supercarrier. Miles away, across the island, she could see the *Osiris* hovering at anchor, an even larger flying megalith than the colossus she presently stood upon. Presumably the *Osiris* crew was engaged in building another beach head there. Major Hummel had the *Osiris* there to support *Projekt Harvest*.

Maria envisioned a world where this was commonplace, where a contingent of Silver Star had merely to arrive and begin conquering while meeting with little resistance anywhere, in any city, on any continent.

She inhaled the warm, tropical air and ducked inside the flight deck to return to her quarters. This would be her finest performance yet. Although disappointed that Crowley would not be here to personally witness her success, she knew he would hear about it. He would feel the reverberations throughout the cosmos.

She would see to it that he knew how powerful she was becoming.

℘

The House of Pain had been left where it stood, a strange memorial to the horrors which had once occurred within its walls. Despite its fearsome moniker, it was simply an old laboratory, filled with broken and rusted scientific equipment from the Victorian era. Just some gray walls, now crumbling and ivy-grown. The roof above the operating theater had caved in long ago, cracked timbers lying undisturbed across the sundered surgery table, its leather restraints having been chewed away by vermin.

Shattered glass beakers and test tubes, chemistry paraphernalia from another time, lay scattered across a dirt-strewn tile floor. The occasional syringe, bone saw, scalpel, or clamp, tarnished and bent, were reminders of the excruciating torture that had happened within this chamber: torture in the name of science. In this room, Moreau had performed experimental surgeries, vivisection, grafting human and animal tissue in an effort to create human-animal hybrids. Some of the experiments had taken root better than others, with certain of the "beast folk" elevated in consciousness to nearly human levels. Still others failed, with some subjects reverting back to a bestial state.

Moreau, British but of French extraction, had been an eminent research scientist, well-known in London society. However his initial experiments in vivisection had become public knowledge, and he was driven from England to Noble's Isle in the middle of the Pacific. Edward Prendick, a rescued castaway, had discovered Moreau's horrible experiments. Often at odds with Moreau and his alcoholic assistant, Dr. Montgomery, Prendick was the only human to survive the fire and beast folk rebellion that destroyed Moreau's entire home and compound, including the House of Pain. Montgomery was killed fighting beast folk, and Moreau in combat with his prized puma woman.

It was a tale passed down these past three generations: of Moreau, the Maker; of Prendick, the Liberator. This history all beast folk knew. The history and the Law, of which the Sayer of the Law constantly reminded them:

Not to go on all-fours; not to suck up Drink; not to eat Fish or Flesh; not to claw the Bark of Trees; not to chase other Men. That is the Law. Are we not Men?

At one time, Moreau had been deified. The beast folk once sang of his power: *His is the House of Pain; his is the Hand that makes; his is the Hand that wounds; his is the Hand that heals; his is the lightning flash; his is the deep, salt sea; his are the stars in the sky.*

That segment of beast folk lore had been abandoned after the great fire that destroyed the compound and the riot that left the House of Pain a ruin. In the time since, other concepts had been added to the Law, while some had been dropped altogether. The eating of fish was no longer prohibited, for example, while living together in communities was strictly governed.

No one dared visit the old compound. It was believed to be haunted, or protected by dark magic. The only one allowed to investigate its secrets was Nariaal, by special dispensation of the Elders and the Sayer of the Law. And now it was Nariaal who pored over the last hand-written journal filled with Moreau's own notes.

The sole surviving supply cabinet had a rusted metal counter top, and various medical texts and notebooks were strewn across its surface. A dark form leaned over the books, reading by lantern light fueled by the flammable mud found in the Burning Bog at the south end of the island. The form shifted, flipping some pages and making notes in another journal. A passerby might have taken the shape for human, but for the 350-pound simian frame and black and gray markings of a male silverback gorilla.

Nariaal sniffed, rubbing away an itch under his nose with the back of a huge index finger. He'd finally located the journal with Moreau's notes regarding the retention of human intellect, and had spent all day into the waning twilight reading it. If this was like any number of Moreau's experiments which Nariaal had replicated at the Fort Sanctuary medical facility, with the proper use of pain management, it could mean a major step forward in the evolution of the beast folk community on the island.

Closing his own notebook, he put the salvaged tomes into a canvas shoulder bag and padded on massive feet to the telephone box at the ruins of Moreau's home at the north end of the compound, planting his torch in the coiled root of a banyan tree he often used for this purpose. He walked upright, lower limbs having been lengthened as a result of third-generation beast folk traits. For what some might deem obvious reasons, the primates in Moreau's experiments had taken more readily and permanently to the introduction of human genetic material and its subsequent influence. Eventually, they'd come to embrace their expanding consciousness and human intellect. Among the beast folk of Sanctuary Island, Nariaal was the analog to Albert Einstein.

The telephone box was rudimentary and three decades out of date, but it worked to connect the compound with Fort Sanctuary and the outlying villages with wiring the ape man had run himself. It was bracketed to a hewn timber, half-charred from the Great Fire, but still strong. The timber thrust up vertically from the ground, a good four feet above the hole in which it was planted. He plucked the earpiece from the cradle and turned the crank on the side, sending a signal through the wires.

"Nariaal to Fort Sanctuary," he growled in a low baritone.

"Fort Sanctuary," said a female voice at the other end of the line. "We hear you, Nariaal."

"Tell the Governor my voyage was successful. I am returning tomorrow. I have also instructed the outlying villages to seek shelter at the fort. The sky invaders are everywhere now."

"Affirmative," came the reply. "Have a safe journey home."

The huge gorilla-man put the earpiece back in the cradle and cocked his head. One half of a massive eyebrow raised, coal-colored irises gleaming in the torchlight. Shaggy silver and black hair raised on the nape of his neck. His giant, flattened nostrils flared as he tested the air. There was something off in the evening breeze. Something that smelled unlike anything he was used to.

A soft snap of twigs caused the ape man to cock his head, wide hand gripping the top of the bag slung over his shoulder. With adrenaline rising, he crouched and prepared to run... or fight.

- CHAPTER 15 -

Captain Hummel reached down to buff the some sand from the toe of his otherwise pristine black boot. Camp had been made, a basic stockade constructed from some of the palm trees along the shoreline. The scent of cooking fires wafted across the beach, carried on a temperate summer breeze.

Looking around, he noted a half dozen sentries, each armed with a submachine gun, walk various patterns near the mouth of the jungle, as engineers felled more timber for the coastal fortification.

Two hundred feet above the beach, the Osiris hovered, straining at her twin anchors, casting a long shadow in the waning daylight.

Hummel currently found himself in a holding pattern. He'd gone from commanding field operations throughout Asia, to supporting the crazed supernatural acquisition project currently being backed by Crowley. He'd heard of that Himmler character before, back in Europe after the war. The delusional designs for capturing demons as a power source were by now common knowledge among the Silver Star. As far as Hummel was concerned, he trusted the man not an inch further than he could throw him.

Yet here he was, raiding the island's local population to supply ready sacrifices for Maria Blutig. In another reality, they might have been friends, or more, instead of rivals for power and station within the Astrum Argentum.

It left a sour taste in his mouth. As a junior officer cranked up a Victrola and folded the stylus down onto a lacquer Louis Armstrong record, filling the beach with the brassy belch of jazz, Hummel briefly considered staying on the beach for the night, finding camaraderie among his soldiers. He slapped a tiny, biting insect from its landing place on his jaw, and suddenly felt the disgust rise like bile in his throat. His mood instantly inverted, and all bets were off. He decided to return to his quarters aboard the *Osiris* and await further commands.

As he turned to flag down the pilot of the gyro skiff, a shout erupted from the jungle, and he spun around to see the squad of scouts he'd dispatched two hours ago herding a strange group of prisoners toward the encampment. Hummel squinted through discerning eyes. The rumors were true. A collection of *actual human-animal hybrids* were walking into his charge—upright on two legs, their very human hands bound in front of them.

There were twenty of them, all dressed in their homespun clothing. The pig-woman elder, her bear mate, the dog-woman, various lesser officials, and one of the ape twins looked nervously about the beach, from the debris fire at the north end of the fortifications to the stockade of palm trees. The only humans they'd ever encountered in the flesh had been the native Kanak, and the Water Soldiers. They'd never seen organization on this scale before—at least not outside their own construction projects, usually under the supervision of Nariaal.

"Stellar work," Hummel praised the lieutenant as he looked them over. "Do any of you speak?"

"We can speak," said a voice, low and quiet. "Are we not men?"

Hummel stifled a laugh. "Decidedly not," he replied. "But who speaks for you?"

The old panther-man raised his head and stepped forward. "I am the Sayer of the Law," he said.

Hummel feigned interest. "The Sayer of the Law, eh? Well, just what is this Law, may I inquire?"

"Not to go on all fours," the old panther replied. "That is the Law. Are we not Men?"

Hummel laughed, his voice dripping with derision. "Again, no. Most assuredly not. And what else?"

"Not to spill blood," came the wizened reply. "You must leave this place."

The lieutenant brought the butt of the MP-18 up into the Speaker's face, coaxing a bloody explosion from his muzzle. The Sayer reached up with bound hands to try to cover his nose, but blood gushed out, staining the white coral sand with a dark spatter.

"Listen carefully, Sayer of the Law," Hummel smiled, his lips thin and reptilian. "You are *not* men, we have no intention of leaving before we are finished here, and *I* say when blood will be spilled..." Hummel caught the Sayer's eye, now swelling with the rifle stock's impact. "And *whose*."

The fronds of an Alocasia plant near the compound exit shivered in place, and Nariaal relaxed. "Come out. I can smell you." As if to punctuate the thought, the great slits of his nostrils flared and contracted as he tested the air, finally cocking his brow in surprise. "Gregor?"

Tentatively, timidly, the fronds of the elephant ear plant parted, and the frightened face of a young ape thrust from the center. "Uncle!"

Nariaal's face showed a complex tapestry of simultaneous emotion. "Gregor, come here," he ordered, pointing a long index finger at a spot on the ground adjacent to his own wide, simian feet.

Gregor was clearly unused to disobedience. Plant leaves rustled and shook violently as the ape child climbed from its green shadows and strode to Nariaal's side. "Uncle! I'm so glad I found you!"

Nariaal swept his young nephew into a tight embrace. "Nephew," he scolded, finally holding Gregor at arm's length, "How came you here? You know it is forbidden to go to the House of Pain without an elder."

Tears began to well in Gregor's huge brown eyes, and his lip trembled. "I didn't know where else to go, Uncle...I know you were leaving the House of Pain today to return to Fort Sanctuary..."

Nariaal set Gregor down on the stone tile of the old atrium, squatting to put his eye level closer to that of his nephew. "Your village was supposed to evacuate to Fort Sanctuary," he said slowly. "Gregor, what happened?"

"The Sky Men..." Gregor began, trailing off with a whimper.

"What about the Sky Men?" Nariaal pressed.

"We did leave the village, as you instructed, Uncle—really we did..."

"Gregor..."

"They came upon us where the road to Fort Santuary crosses the eastern trail to the sea."

"You say the *eastern* trail?" Nariaal's brow furrowed as he made geographical calculations. "Then that means there are two camps."

Gregor nodded. "The camp Neela saw was on the western coast, but these soldiers took us east. Some have said there are two great sky ships over our island, though I have not seen one yet."

Nariaal continued, trying to get the pertinent facts from his young nephew. "How many were captured?"

Gregor wiggled his fingers and toes, silently counting the digits. "Twenty. They took my brother, and most of the elders, and the Sayer of the Law."

"And what happened to the others?"

Gregor shivered in his homespun tunic. He clamped his eyes shut at the prospect of revisiting the scene. "Some tried to defend the elders," he croaked, almost in a whisper. "The soldiers shot them with guns." The young ape recounted the story, the fur on his cheeks matted with tears. "So much blood, Uncle..."

Nariaal closed his own eyes and sighed. "The Old Law does not apply to defending one's own life, or the lives of others. And I fear much more blood will be spilled here before Sanctuary is rid of these Sky Men." Nariaal's brow arced in surprise as he made a sudden connection with something Gregor had said. "You said the soldiers took *us* east? Were you taken prisoner with them?"

Gregor cast a look down at his wide feet, almost ashamed. "Yes, Uncle. But I escaped into the jungle. So did Neela, but she went a different way..."

Nariaal was suddenly frantic. "Gregor. Climb on my back. Now."

Without a moment's hesitation, the young ape scampered up the silver-haired back of his elder.

"Hold on tightly."

Nariaal felt his nephew's fingers grip the fur at his shoulders with a strength and tenacity that belied his age and relative size. He turned to the atrium wall just as an entire line of Alocasia bushes erupted in the thrashing of jungle fatigues and the stomping of jackboots. Both apes heard the ratcheting back of submachine gun bolts, but Nariaal was at the top of the wall and leaping into the blackness of the jungle as the first shots peppered the atrium, tearing through the great tree trunk, and shredding the telephone box and the post from which it had once hung.

☙

All was ready.

The beach fortifications had been completed earlier in the day, and Maria had insisted that a night of the new moon would be the perfect opportunity to test the ritual. If it worked, she might manage three summonings before requiring to rest. And even so, Maria had previously demonstrated the ability to siphon the life energy from another human being, replenishing what she lost while powering her own complex magicks.

The central altar had already been prepared with the demonic entrapment device on the upper platform, while the summoning alcove and technician's station currently remained vacant. When they began the ritual, Mr. Himmler would take his position there, while Maria would enter the relative safety of the alcove. An elevated holding cell was also currently vacant, but soon would hold up to four individuals for demonic consumption. The stockade pen of living sacrifices lay a few paces to the north. Fires roiled and flickered in large metal braziers: two on the main altar, one next to the pen, four across the stockade wall, and four more planted along the beach to supply light for the Silver Star soldiers in their duties.

There were at the moment four units of commandos on the beach, six soldiers in each unit. One unit was deployed as a security detail for the prisoners when walking from the holding pen to the altar. Another two were each stationed at the north and south ends of the beach head. The last unit was stationed at the top of the picket wall.

The wall itself was fifteen feet tall, sporting a semi-enclosed guard tower at each end and a smaller cutout door in its center, facing a large trail which led into the jungle. The unit of troops at the wall had been split into two heavy machine gun teams of two men each, who occupied the guard towers, and whose hardware was currently facing out toward the jungle interior. They could be shifted to focus on the altar and the beach, if necessary. The remaining two soldiers patrolled the top of the picket wall, with submachine guns and electric halogen searchlights, keeping hostiles out and sacrifices in.

Maria Blutig stood on the sun-bleached coral sand of her tropical paradise, dressed in the robes of an Astrum Argentum high priestess. Almost six feet tall and draped in layers of gray and deep royal purple, she cut an imposing figure, especially when she donned the miter cap richly embroidered in mystical symbols whose meaning was only known to Silver Star mystics and their cult.

Six of these cultists stood around Maria in a semicircle. They wore robes of a similar style and materials, but of demonstrably lower rank and station.

Noticeably absent on the beach was Captain Ecke, commander sof the *Luftpanzer II*, who had in recent months become hesitant when it came to the supernatural portion of Silver Star's mission. Ecke had been an airship commander in the Great War, responsible for destroying half of London. Now white-bearded and cynical, he nonetheless remained a military man. All he wanted to do was command his airship and collect some money for his pension. Political intrigue and summoning demons were far outside his comfort zone.

"*Herr* Himmler," Maria barked. "Let us begin!"

The bespectacled scientist nodded, tying on the leather mechanic's apron he'd been using for twenty years. "*Jawohl*," he nodded, striding across the beach from the landing zone to the altar.

He had to admit, his engineering brain appreciated the craftsmanship of the altar construction. The Silver Star knew how to build a fortification out of native materials, sure. But the altar was definitely impressive in its own right.

Taking up his position at the foot of the raised dais, he inspected the switch box nailed to a vertical palm log support. The one-by-two-foot metal rectangle housed the transformer that took incoming electricity from the diesel generator on the beach and powered the demon trap housing on the platform above. Currently the power indicator shone a steady green, and the lever was locked in the down position. He flicked open the locking mechanism and flashed Maria a thumb's up. *"Alles gut!"*

Maria pointed toward the prisoner pen with a slender finger. "Bring forth two sacrifices!" she ordered, watching as three well-armed commandos muscled two of the strapping Kanak braves out of the holding area and shoved them toward the ladder that led up to the elevated cage.

Still bound at the wrists, one of the native men stumbled and fell in the warm sand. The other took advantage of the confusion to run at the cutout door in the picket wall. Sun-tanned limbs flexed and sprang as he sprinted toward freedom. As soldiers all over the beach shouted and rallied their attention toward the would-be escapee, the two commandos atop the midsection of the wall trained their MP-18s downward and began to fire at the sand below. The Kanak man was able to take two running rams at the door—nudging the wooden deadbolt aside on his second try—before getting peppered with bullets and falling to the ground, his blood staining the sand dark crimson as his life slipped away.

Without missing a beat, two commandos dragged the body away toward the water, and the soldiers monitoring the prisoners in the stockade returned and pulled one of the two women from within.

Maria smiled knowingly. Her soldiers were not only well-trained to anticipate her every whim, but scared to death of crossing her in any way. She entered the mage's chamber beneath the elevated dais, took a deep breath, and began to enter a trance-like state.

Her acolytes knelt in their semicircle around the entry to the chamber, leaning hooded heads forward and beginning to chant in low tones.

The security detail wrestled their Kanak prisoners into the elevated cage, barring the door behind them. One of the soldiers at the bottom of the ladder announced, "Prisoners secure."

Without wasting any time, Maria thrust her arms out, palms open to the sand beneath her feet. "Powers of darkness and mystery," she began, "I call upon thee!"

The hooded heads dropped as the acolytes bowed in supplication. The low drone from six throats reverberated into the hollow mage chamber.

"Elder gods of the dark universe before and after time," Maria continued, "I call upon thee!"

Himmler stood at the ready, his hand on the lever switch.

"Denizens of the eldritch dimension *Narakam*, hear me. Feel my power and take heed. I summon a single demon-form of the *shayatin*—come forth into this world and feed!"

As it happened in a warm August night in Paris seven years ago, the air above the dais began to pulse and crackle with electricity. A miniature storm cloud built upon itself and throbbed into existence, almost like a black demonic heart.

The chorus of cultists knelt in the sand and swayed in a trance of their own, repeating:

Shayatin, shayatin, come forth and feed!

Shayatin, shayatin, come forth and feed!

The cloud above the altar pulsed and instantly doubled in size, and tendrils of static electricity probed the dais from within the storm.

"Heed me, *shayatin*," Maria ordered. "Come forth and feed."

Shayatin, shayatin, come forth and feed!

The chants of the acolytes were suddenly overtaken and replaced by the low-pitched thrum of otherworldly energies. The roiling ectoplasmic storm bulged like an arachnid egg sac, and the first long, spindly digit probed out through the breech.

Maria hadn't been in Paris that night, but she'd read the report, and knew her ritual could maintain better control of whatever poked its otherworldly head out of its otherworldly home. She kept her concentration focused on the storm above her head, coaxing, pulling the eldritch creature through the amniotic membrane between dimensions.

The fabric of space and time tore open along the surgical wound Maria's ritual had created, and the unholy creature dropped to the dais on four grotesque limbs. Four black insectoid eyes shone from the equally black body, its shape almost spider-like yet veiny and rippling with alien musculature. The drooling maw opened in anticipation. The thing was ready to feed.

Screams erupted from inside the sacrificial cage, as the prisoners looked upon the face, if it could be reasonably called such, of the creature from beyond their reality.

The low thrum continued to vibrate from the very air around the beach, and suddenly the screams ceased with an asphyxiated wheeze as the creature pulled their life force away, feeding on their fear and their helplessness, their hopes and dreams, their innocence. The sinewy body, now bloated and full, sagged between the claw-tipped spindle legs.

"Now!" Maria ordered, and Himmler flipped the lever and opened the trap doors in his device. A single arc of electricity rocketed up from the open box to grab the creature like a shimmering blue-white hand.

He then flipped the switch to the closed position, and the demon was impelled into the jaws of the device. The storm dissipated as quickly as it had begun, and suddenly the ritual was over.

Himmler rushed to the stack of traps and grabbed a fresh one, then climbed the ladder to the dais. He peeked inside the sacrificial cage and noted that the Kanak man and woman were in fact dead. Both appeared pale, dessicated husks of their former selves.

Himmler knelt by the used device and unscrewed the wing nuts that secured the electrical and control leads from the workstation below, replacing it with the new device and securing it in the same fashion.

The German engineer climbed down from the dais and peered into the mage chamber. Maria seemed slightly fatigued, but stood strongly on her feet, her bare toes gripping and releasing the sand beneath her priestly gowns. "The capture has been successful!" he announced. "The second device has been prepared!"

Maria smiled. "I am ready. Bring two more sacrifices."

- CHAPTER 16 -

Rivets couldn't see the majority of what had just occurred on the beach, but he'd sure heard plenty of it. And he was able to witness the Kanak man's desperate break for freedom at the cut-in door in the picket wall. The small detail he'd noticed—one which apparently nobody else had—was the wooden deadbolt. Specifically, that it was halfway open. The commandos who had arrived to drag the dead native's body away hadn't noticed, and hadn't fixed the issue. The guards on the wall were too high up to see it, and Maria's contingent was too far distant and facing away from the wall to begin with.

There just happened to be a wide enough vertical split between two of the logs in the stockade, which just happened to be facing the center of the wall where the door was placed, and which Rivets just happened to be next to when the escape attempt occurred.

The whole event started the weary wheels in his mind turning again. He'd been in a Silver Star stockade before, in the Amazon jungle, awaiting sacrifice to an elder demon that Crowley himself attempted to summon. A summoning thankfully thwarted by Doc and a 16th century holy relic. He didn't like being in a Silver Star stockade. At least in a holding cell or an interrogation center, he knew he was worth something.

He'd already managed to loosen the sisal rope bindings around his wrists; it would only take a quick twist of the wrist to shed them. And then? And then, grab a weapon from one of the soldiers and get to the door as quickly as possible, hoping for plenty of cover in the deep jungle and the dark night.

It was a garbage plan, he knew it. But it was all he had. And Rivets had the benefit of having survived until now on the back of more than one garbage plan.

"I am ready. Bring two more sacrifices," came the order from Maria at the altar. "Make sure that Commander Holloway is one of them."

Rivets' gut seized up and he suddenly felt nauseous. He saw the holding pen door swing open, and a gray-uniformed soldier shoved his way in past the ten or so natives at the front of the stockade. Rivets put on his best haggard look to put the soldier off his guard—not that a haggard look was much of a stretch after almost a month in Silver Star custody.

As the soldier reached him, grabbing Rivets by the collar of his stained work shirt, he suddenly knew how he'd work his escape: the soldier pulled with a great deal of force, as he anticipated Rivets to be sluggish and slow. It would have been a good guess on most days, with most people. Instead of resisting, Rivets pushed forward with the soldier's pull, knocking him off balance. As the two stumbled forward, Rivets pulled the rope from his wrists, resulting in a large loop of sisal still gripped in his left hand. Instantly the rope went around the soldier's neck, and as the man's head snapped back, both of his hands followed to the source of trauma, and he dropped the submachine gun. Rivets snapped it up in his right hand before it hit the ground.

No one was expecting the chaos that followed.

Not Maria, in her almost ecstatic magic-induced trance. Not the acolytes kneeling at her feet. Not Himmler, at his science station below the altar. Not the four units of Silver Star commandos on the beach.

By the time the soldier outside the stockade door realized what was going on, he'd been knocked to his back by the combined mass of Rivets and the soldier he was strangling. His head impacted an exposed section of lava rock and he lost consciousness. Almost immediately, his face began to wither and sag, his body sizzling and smoking with decay.

Rivets staggered backward, whipping the MP-18 up to access the bolt with his left hand, which was holding the soldier's throat with the rope. He slammed the side of the weapon into the soldier's head, and was able to pull back the bolt on the second attempt, but left the soldier with a bloody gash in his right temple.

The other eight Kanak burst from the stockade, hands still bound, but determined to escape if possible. One of the men picked up the fallen guard's belt knife and used it to cut the bindings off some of the escapees.

One of the women picked up the fallen guard's MP-18 and pointed it at the soldiers on the wall. Immediately she, and the native man with the knife, were gunned down by the sentries on the wall.

Another Kanak woman ran and leaped into the sea, disappearing under the four-foot surf.

Searchlights scanned after her, and heavy machine guns shifted positions within the guard towers. Natives scrambled on the beach, sprinting either north or south, but to no avail.

It was now or never.

Rivets struggled with the semi-conscious guard, dragging him backward toward the wall. With the guards' focus on the chaos farther out on the beach, he dug into the sand and pushed for the door. Within just a handful of paces, his back was against the deadbolt. He pressed back and to his left, using his weight in combination with the soldier to slide the deadbolt out of position. The deadbolt's position on the inside of the wall indicated the door also opened inward. Having slid free of the door itself, Rivets nudged it open with the barrel of the stolen gun.

Mustering all of his strength and pulling the soldier upright by the neck, Rivets found himself in a figurative pickle. The man was already purple, and a small plume of acrid smoke began to trail up out of his mouth and nose. He knew taking a Silver Star hostage was generally not good leverage. They tended to literally fall apart when caught, and only in the rarest cases were ransomed back. Even if Rivets' only intention was to use this guy as a human shield, a few more seconds and he wouldn't even be useful for that.

Thinking quickly, Rivet's untwisted the twine around his captive's throat, shoving the body down into the sand as he ducked out through the door.

In front of him lay a jungle path into the dark. Behind him was certain death. The shouts of surprise and anger were the perfect cover. Hunching over to run as fast as his old wounded legs could carry him, Rivets sprinted toward the first expanse of palms and acacia trees.

It was too late. The searchlights had found him.

He was only ten yards into the jungle when he heard the stutter of automatic gunfire and felt the bullets tear into his flesh.

ↂ

As ship chronometers and crew watches ticked past 0800 the next morning, The *Percival* and *Daedalus* loomed like giant, silvery sharks over the shimmering blue Pacific. Below them, the blasted remains of a tropical paradise lay scattered among the reefs and shallows. It looked to have been a volcanic cataclysm that made the mess. The fragments of a once-majestic mountain now lay strewn about the vicinity, larger pieces jutting up from the sandy sea floor like the teeth of some massive aquatic beast.

Whatever happened here had occurred generations ago; the island fragments had been re-seeded by birds and were now nesting platforms for terns, gulls, and plovers. The clear, shallow water between outcroppings created a labyrinth of fertile bedding for oysters and crustaceans, the rays and skates that fed on them, and the reef sharks that fed on the rays and skates. One small section of the original tail of the island remained above water, a tiny spit of white sand and a small grove of coconut palms, insufficient for any kind of aerial moorage.

On the *Daedalus* bridge, Jack throttled down to station-keeping, holding altitude at two hundred feet. He gazed out at the shattered island below them, brow furrowing. "Well, here we are. And what did this used to be, I wonder?"

"Part of Maria Theresa Reef, perhaps?" Doc offered.

Cipher looked over Jack's shoulder out the bridge window array. "This used to be an island," she said cryptically.

"Cipher, patch me through to *Percival*," Jack ordered.

Cipher swapped a patch cord into a small receptacle on her console and flipped a switch. "*Percival* patched in, Captain."

Jack hit the *TALK* button on his headset. "*Daedalus* to *Percival*. Hang back a hundred meters or so. I'm taking her down for a closer look." Flipping the toggles for ballonets 1 and 2, Jack caused the release of hydrogen-helium lift gas from the valves, and the ship began to nose down and drop slowly.

Doc opened a book containing archaic charts and maps of "lost" places, searching for any reference to an exploded tropical island at their location. They were too far from Krakatoa, which was probably the most famous volcanic explosion in modern history, perhaps since the destruction of Santorini or Pompeii.

"Here," she said, leaning over the nav console to read from the tome. "Lincoln Island, discovered by Cyrus Smith in 1865. Smith and party were rescued by the ship *Duncan* shortly after the volcano erupted in 1869."

"Imagine riding out an eruption large enough to destroy the island," Jack marveled, "with only that small spit of solid ground to cling to." He fired up the turbofans and pivoted around the nose of the ship, scouring the shallow water for clues. As he rounded a large rock thrust up from the ocean floor, he saw the white sand give way to a deep well. It was filled with boulders both large and small, and a shape resembling a large propeller screw, now bent and encrusted with barnacles and coral. "There's something in that hole, dead center of the island...or where the island used to be," said Jack.

"What do you think it is?" Doc asked, intrigued.

"Hard to say," Jack squinted. He whirled the ship around with the nose angled toward the well, but far enough away to see everything within. That put the belly of the *Daedalus* less than a hundred feet above the ocean's surface, on the side of the island that abruptly fell into deeper water.

Just as Jack was steadying the ship's pitch, the sea beneath them began to roil and froth like a boiling pot. A shape like that of a giant metal swordfish broke the surface, long lance point cresting first, followed by a slender, torpedo-shaped nose. As the forward third of the craft came down on the water with a rush of white foam, more of the dorsal area hove into view. It was perhaps six hundred feet long from tip to tail, close to a hundred feet abeam, and of a more cylindrical design than the knife-shaped U-boats from the Great War. Copper-clad and blue-green patinaed, she sported a forward bridge set above a pair of fin-shaped steering planes. A flat metal top deck with railing ran from just behind the forward bridge to a point short of the tail assembly. A single ship's boat, also of metal construction, was secured to the top deck, slightly forward of the aft hatch. A giant circular window, bubble-shaped and yellow, stared out from each side amidships, like the baleful eye of a giant sea creature.

Jack angled up and back from the breaching submarine, watching through the windows as the aft hatch opened and crewmen in dark pants and blue and white striped shirts spilled onto the top deck. They seemed mostly male, dark in skin tone with the exception of a couple of lighter-skinned Asian or European individuals.

Cipher's radio receiver began to crackle, and a female voice chattered something in Hindi. She put her hand to the earphones, taking in the contact and preparing to translate. "Captain, I have the submarine commander. She requests lowing a mooring cable to effect a meeting."

Jack nodded. Things were about to get very interesting. He hit his *TALK* button. "Deadeye and Asim, ready a mooring cable from the aft winch." Taking his finger off the headset, he turned in his seat toward the comms station. "Cipher, acknowledge and let the submarine know we will winch down to them once they've secured our mooring cable."

The *Daedalus* descended over the back of the submarine, of a scale that rivaled each of the airships hovering above. While Jack kept her steady in the air, Deadeye and Asim lowered a steel mooring cable, hook dangling from the loose end. One of the submarine crewmen snagged the cable with a boarding gaff, and three of them wrapped it around a deck cleat, securing the hook back onto the cable. When the signal was given, Deadeye switched the winch on, and the ship began to crawl downward.

Jack shut down the engines and shrugged out of the seat harness.

"And where do you think you're going?" Doc asked, hands on hips.

"The submarine commander wants to effect a meeting. I'm going to meet her."

"Captain," Cipher raised an index finger as if petitioning a teacher for attention. "The submarine's commander speaks native Hindi. Permission to come along."

"Granted," Jack nodded. He wasn't about to debate Cipher on this one.

Doc wasn't satisfied. "But what if...?"

"Look. If anything goes wrong, we'll need the most experienced officer available to take command. That's you, like it or not." Jack grabbed her by the shoulders and planted a firm kiss on her mouth. "We'll be fine," he smiled, heading through the bridge doorway toward the aft hatch. Doc fumed, but took a deep breath and exhaled, relaxing her posture. As it was, there was no one left on the bridge to vent her ire upon.

Cipher followed, checking the cylinder on her sidearm: full and ready.

They arrived at the hatch, Deadeye having lowered the aluminum chain ladder already. Asim stood next to the hatch, and Sparks emerged from the engine room to observe the goings on.

"Asim," said Jack, "go forward and take the helm. Keep engines powered down, but be ready for anything."

The young pilot saluted and headed toward the front of the craft. "*Naqeeb.*"

As Jack prepared to step down onto the ladder, he clapped Deadeye on the shoulder. "Keep an eye open, will ya? Stay alert."

"You betcha," Charlie answered. "Be careful."

Jack clambered down some twenty-five feet to the dorsal top deck of the submarine, Cipher following close behind. The crew was much as Jack had surmised from a distance: mostly of east Indian or Micronesian extraction, with the exception of a couple of crewmen from China or southeast Asia.

The aft deck hatch lay open, and presently filled with something Jack had not been expecting. A massive bovine head thrust up through the open portal—a clear six inches of cattle horn sprouting from each side of the great skull—followed by a well-muscled human torso. If there was a modern equivalent for the classical Minotaur of Greek legend, this was it. The crewman was ostensibly human in every way, save for the ox head and horns, and a tough gray-brown cowhide skin. Standing close to seven feet tall, he wore the same dark trousers and blue and white short--sleeved shirt as the other crewmen, with a matching kerchief and garrison cap. He looked like he'd have no problem ridding the boat of any potential threats with his broad, bare hands. Or perhaps a head butt from those horns.

Jack and Cipher exchanged a look of bewilderment, but didn't have long to gawk at the man as he took a position on the right side of the deck.

A woman wearing an officer's cover and smart naval duty uniform appeared at the hatch, and climbed out into the sunlight. She was perhaps five-foot-eight, with amber eyes, skin the hue and tone of rich brown clay. Ears were pierced with multiple hoops of yellow gold, she carried a saber in a scabbard at her hip. A wide, black belt bisected her outfit, from the white turtleneck and open blue jacket on top, to the tight blue leggings and black knee boots below. Long, raven tresses had been braided in back. Only a shock of hair dropped beneath the cap's bill across her forehead.

She strode toward her visitors without pause, eyes afire with apprehension. "You are Captain Stratosphere," she said in a clipped Hindi accent, her hand outstretched. Jack shook it.

"Jack McGraw," he said. "This is my communication's officer, Lieutenant Marissa Singh."

The submarine captain looked Cipher up and down, appraising her. She smiled intently, never relaxing her guard. "I am Nemo," she said. "Welcome aboard the *Nautilus*."

- CHAPTER 17 -

"I don't trust easily," Nemo admitted, peering at Jack from the shade of her cap. "I hope you realize the risk I am taking."

"Did you sink a British freighter and war ship in the Philippine Sea?" Jack asked directly.

"I make no apologies for attacking the shipping of colonial powers," she frowned. "And if you insist on this line of questioning, the trust I mentioned will never come to be."

"Apologies," Cipher interjected. "My captain is a man of action, which can seem blunt at times."

Jack flashed a look of incredulity at Cipher, who returned with one of her own.

"You are Punjabi?" Nemo queried.

"Yes," Cipher replied. "Although educated abroad."

"Let me guess. Oxford."

Cipher blinked in disbelief. The woman was absolutely right.

Jack shifted in the hot sun on the top deck. "You said your name was Nemo. Any relation to the Nemo who attacked all those ships in the 1860s?"

"Prince Dakkar was my grandfather," she said, casting a downward glance.

"I'd always heard his ship, the *Nautilus*, was lost at sea."

"Not lost," said Nemo. "You saw her resting place in the grotto."

Cipher was shocked. "In the center of the island?"

"He stayed as the island tore itself apart," she replied, "and is buried with the original *Nautilus*. This vessel is uniquely my design."

"Beautiful ship, Captain," Jack said, nodding, "and you have our attention."

"Very good, 'man of action'," Nemo winked. "You will be my guests on this leg of the voyage." She bowed, gesturing toward the open hatch. "Kindly radio your ships to follow. We will not submerge unless necessary."

Jack tensed. "Hang on—"

"Captain," Cipher whispered, nudging him in the ribs, "we are *guests*, not hostages."

Jack took a deep breath and nodded. "Right. Sorry." Turning to face the airship cabled to the submarine, he waved to Asim in the cockpit. As they moved toward the hatch, Jack saw the deck crew rushing to and fro, and one crewman stopped to unhook the *Daedalus'* tether cable from the railing.

Jack marveled at the efficiency of this multinational, almost certainly multi-species crew, as he and Cipher were invited below and the ship made for departure. He'd toured a U-boat once during the war, but this vehicle was unlike any currently at sea...or under it.

The top deck was positioned two thirds of the way back, just before the hatch door to the engine room, so as they descended the metal stairs Jack expected to smell diesel fuel and piston grease. But there was no hint, no petroleum odor, and no telltale growl of internal combustion engines. As they came to the main deck that ran throughout the ship, Cipher touched his shoulder to get his attention.

"Captain," she said. "No diesel fumes. No petrol smell at all."

Jack nodded, already several miles down that mental trail. "The *Nautilus* must be electric," he surmised.

"Indeed she is," Nemo smiled proudly, leading them forward as the ship began to get underway. They paused at a radio comms station and Jack was handed a headset consisting of earphones and a single microphone on an arm extending from the left earpiece.

Jack donned the headset and leaned over the console, pressing a rectangular *TALK* button. "McGraw to airships *Daedalus* and *Percival*. Form up at two hundred feet and follow the *Nautilus* to its destination. Flotilla command transferred to Commander Willis until rendezvous. *Daedalus*, prepare to detach."

Doc replied, a tremor of worry in her voice. "Acknowledged. What is the away party's status?"

Jack pressed the button again. "We're okay, Doc. Just along for the ride. See you soon."

When the *Percival* signaled affirmative, Jack passed the headset back to the Indian radio operator, and he and Cipher fell in behind Nemo.

Only a slight whine of electric motors could be heard as multiple screws began to churn the water behind the great ship, and Jack could feel the sensation of forward movement. Nemo led them forward to a small bridge which consisted of several stations arranged in a circle around a central command platform. A bearded Indian sailor manned depth control, an Arab woman sat at weapons control, and a crewman with pronounced canine features monitored underwater sound through a set of ASDIC hydrophones. The conning tower, such as it was, lay just behind a triangular wedge protrusion of steel and reinforced glass view ports, through which the sole pilot, a slender Bengali boy of not more than 18, could see ahead. The ship's controls consisted of an old fashioned nautical steering wheel of polished aluminum fitted with teak and brass accents, which controlled the yaw, while hydroplane controls at the adjacent station controlled the trim.

Though impressed at the technological marvel in front of him, Jack nonetheless found himself preferring the control systems of the aircraft he'd flown. One pilot controlling every maneuvering system was more his idea of efficiency.

Nemo motioned to Jack and Cipher to pause on the main deck while she climbed the perforated metal stairway to the command platform. She strode directly to the chart table and pointed at a position on the map. "Course set for Tabor Island?"

"Yes, Captain!" replied the navigation officer, a woman with feline features and jaguar markings in her fur.

"Abesh," Nemo addressed the pilot, "full speed ahead."

The young helmsman nodded. "Aye, Captain," he said, throwing the brass thrust lever all the way forward on its hinge.

Satisfied, Nemo stepped down from the command center and rejoined her guests. "If you will follow me, please?"

Jack and Cipher followed Nemo forward to a large observation lounge, where a colossal round window graced each side of the ship, looking like the great eyes of a giant squid. Benches upholstered in red crushed velvet were situated back-to-back in a straight line down the center of the submarine, so that a viewer could gaze out the great porthole of whichever side they chose. Jack could see the ocean floor ahead of them drop away into the depths, and although the *Nautilus* remained at the surface, to see the world fall away into darkness like that triggered a primal fear somewhere in his psyche. A pod of dolphins joined the ship, cavorting in front of the giant glass eye as they were challenged to keep up with the speed of the sub.

"I must say," Jack sighed, "she's an impressive piece of work. But I really have to know..."

"Why we contacted you?" Nemo interrupted, running her long braid through a work-worn hand before replacing it behind her neck. Cipher noticed her fingers carried a roadmap of assorted scars, likely from manual labor underwater, among coral and barnacles and any number of sharp, serrated edges.

"If you don't mind," Jack said impatiently.

Cipher gritted her teeth. She loved Captain McGraw as a friend and compatriot, and respected him as a captain, but he was the last person who she'd trust with a sensitive diplomatic matter. Years of fighting in Europe in the war, followed by years of fighting the Silver Star, had put him on high alert. He tended to shoot first and forget about asking questions later.

Nemo was a silhouette in the window, a shadow puppet to the blue world outside. "Word has come to us of AEGIS and their exploits in Africa and the Amazon. We have heard great things about Captain Stratosphere and his champions of the light in combating the growing darkness."

"To what do you refer?" Cipher interjected.

Nemo leveled a severe look at her. "Do not insult us both with that question. The darkness purveyed by those who wish to control all."

"It's okay, Cipher," said Jack. "The fact that we are in a struggle to the death with the Astrum Argentum is not really a secret."

Nemo turned to gaze out of the port-side window, watching a school of skipjack wheel and turn with a silvery flourish, disappearing into the deep. "When we heard that you interceded on behalf of the Kikuyu in Kenya, we knew you were not just another shadowy paramilitary group sponsored by the British-American war machine."

Jack had never heard of the allied powers of Britain and America referred to in those terms. It set him on his heels. "Now hold on, sister..."

"Captain McGraw, my grandfather lost everything he had to the British. His kingdom, his family, everything. His failure in the Rebellion of 1857 made him an international outlaw. He spent the rest of his life nationless, yet in harmony with the sea, fighting injustice and exploitation wherever he found it. The pearl industry. The spice trade. The slave trade. Any who would take territory by force, extract the wealth of a native people with no regard for their welfare, became his enemy. He saw the evils of greed and empire, and he fought both to his dying breath. It is now my honor *and* my duty to continue that struggle."

Cipher replayed the events of their Kenyan travels in her mind: the sight of her countrymen being used to slaughter Kikuyu tribespeople, including a local chief and the father of a woman she now called a friend and crew-mate. Cipher been raised in a pro-British family of privileged social standing, educated in England. But this tour of duty had shaken her to the roots.

"Is that why you took your grandfather's name?" Jack asked.

"Nemo is the Latin rendering of *'outis'* from the Greek. It means 'nobody'. And as long as we fight the oppression of others, we remain nameless, a nation unto ourselves."

Jack began to like the sound of what Nemo was saying. He, too, had his worldview's foundation challenged ever since the war. While he considered himself a patriotic American, he certainly wasn't blind to the evils of colonialism. "How can we help?" he asked.

"You may have noticed some of my crew are a bit...bestial."

"Yes, I was hoping to get around to asking you..."

"They are descendants of a horrible scientific experiment gone awry. The experiment to merge human and animal, perpetrated by the British vivisectionist called Moreau."

Cipher nodded. "I've heard of him."

Nemo turned to face her guests, no longer gazing through the giant eye. "They exist through no fault of their own. And for the past two generations, they have had a peaceful existence on Sanctuary, what the old charts call Noble's Isle. The local Kanak people are the only human souls who know of their existence —besides me and my crew, of course."

"You are their protector," Cipher realized.

"Four days ago, I began to receive reports of two large aircraft in the vicinity of Sanctuary. Soon it was confirmed that it was an invasion force."

Jack's eyes widened. "Two large aircraft?" he growled. "How large, exactly?"

"Larger even than the *Nautilus*, by all reports. They've been landing troops and taking prisoners—"

"We're in," Jack stood, suddenly intent.

"I'm sorry?"

"We'll help you."

Nemo stared back at the tall, scruff-bearded pilot and locked onto his piercing blue eyes.

Jack returned the look and balled his hands into fists. "Help you fight them," he added with intensity.

"We'll be at my base at Tabor Island in about an hour," Nemo said. "At that time, we'll discuss strategy. In the meantime, tell me all you can about this *Astrum Argentum*."

Nemo's port at Tabor Island was a wonder of tactical genius and engineering. As the combined flotilla approached from the northwest, they saw what could only be called "nondescript"—a typical South Seas fishing and trading port, with a tiny harbor half full of fishing sloops and outrigger canoes. Thatched huts and vendor stalls lined the harbor boardwalk, and a dirt path led up a gently curving hillside, which crowded ever more with constructions of bamboo and stone. A large building of unknown purpose sat atop the ridge of the hill, peering out over the island on all sides. The hillside itself had apparently been the outer wall of a volcano at one time, but the fire which had built the island had long gone out, and erosion of sea and wind had done the rest.

Jack and Cipher looked out through the bridge windows as they approached the island at an easy clip. As the submarine cut through the water, Jack began to worry that they were coming into the harbor far too quickly. He and Cipher exchanged a nervous glance, and Jack's eyes bulged when he heard Nemo give the order to dive.

"But I thought—?"

"Do not fear, Captain," Nemo offered with a slight smile at his discomfort. "This dive is absolutely necessary."

A ship's bell erupted behind them in a rapid series of clangs, and a wash of sea foam swirled in front of the viewport. The interior shifted to red lantern light. The *Nautilus* vanished beneath the surface, leaving a small wake of bubbles and froth behind.

Aboard the *Daedalus*, Doc watched from the comms station as the submarine dropped deeper into the water. Because of their altitude and the crystal clarity of the ocean in these parts, the Nautilus remained visible as it dove. Trusting that Nemo wouldn't bring them all the way out here only to kill them, she chose to focus on their landing instructions as they made a wide, high pass overhead.

At the center of the island was a vast lagoon or grotto, surrounded by a white sand beach, upon which the local inhabitants set about their business, cultivating oyster beds about thirty feet down. Some herded varieties of fish into handmade corrals of marine rope—which meant there had to be an opening to the ocean itself somewhere under the surface.

"Single engine," Nemo ordered. "Slow to one-quarter speed."

"Single engine, one-quarter speed, aye!" came the reply of the helmsman.

As the submarine silently propelled itself beneath the fishing boats in the harbor, Jack saw a large cavern opening in the tide-worn pumice of the island's foundation. He'd expected a simple tie-up at the docks, but Nemo had apparently wanted to impress her visitors.

They passed through a narrow lava tube that only left perhaps six feet of clearance on either side. Then sunlight returned, and they were suddenly in a huge lagoon, with white sand and coral reefs creating a tropical aquarium effect. The lake itself was almost perfectly bowl-shaped, and as the submarine cut through its center, rising from the depths of the lava tube, Jack and Cipher watched pearl divers and spear-fishermen kick toward the surface—not out of fear or any sense of danger, but almost a casual regard.

At the far end of the lagoon sat what appeared from the outside to be a jumble of boulders, perhaps chunks of the dead volcano that had slid down from a higher point and come to rest on the beach. However, Jack's vantage on the *Nautilus* bridge provided a look into a narrow opening in the rocks that revealed a perfectly-sized slip and dry dock facility, with gantries leading to a masterfully-constructed wooden stairway leading up the back ridge of the former volcano.

As they disembarked the Nautilus and began the climb to the top gantry, Jack pointed out some features of interest to Cipher: several heavy weapon emplacements had been carved out of the volcano wall, both inside and outside, and Jack could see military surplus field artillery pieces hidden underneath swathes of camouflage netting.

Two large warehouses crouched on the east side of the island, at the bottom of the weathered volcano wall. They weren't aerodromes like the AEGIS crews were used to, like Moffett Field in California, but they were big enough to contain the airships and protect them from the elements, which was more than they'd had even in the Philippines.

After half an hour of landing and docking logistics, various technical inspections and reunions, the crews of the *Daedalus* and *Percival* assembled in what might have been called a "great hall" in medieval times. A structure built from the oak timbers and teak bracings of salvaged shipping, the hall was a massive place for gathering and feasting, and in some cases, like this one, strategic planning.

Glass windows looked out over the island from every angle, and most were hinged at the top to be braced open for airflow. Long teak tables and stools lined either side. Giant standards of blue canvas fabric with Nemo's seal—

a silver N within a circle—hung from the gallery walls. There was no question as to who was in charge on this island. This was truly an eagle's nest worthy of a pirate queen, and Nemo was given the same deference.

But theirs was not the functional democratic utopia of 18th century pirates, with elected captains and disability insurance and a vote in every matter. There was definitely a system of military rank among the Nautilus crew and the wider support organization, and absolutely no doubt regarding who was in charge. If Nemo was indeed a pirate by the English definition, she and her crew behaved far more like an organized navy, with their clean uniforms and battle standard. The irony being that their very identity was predicated on not having one.

As the combined crews gathered around, Nemo stepped behind a large chart table which had been constructed of a deck grate atop an enormous capstan, probably once used to raise ship anchors. Upon the table top were spread a variety of nautical charts and maps of an island Jack and his fellow AEGIS personnel had never seen before.

"This," said Nemo, pointing at the map dead center of the table, "is Sanctuary. No one beyond myself, my crew, and the native inhabitants know of its existence." She looked directly at Jack. "Until now."

Jack nodded, and Nemo continued.

"I was not sure whether to trust you with this, but as they say, 'the enemy of my enemy is my friend'. I maintain AEGIS supports an imperialist agenda, but right now, the Silver Star poses a direct and dangerous threat to all life on the island. And who knows what will happen if they locate our base here?"

"They'll destroy it," Jack announced matter-of-factly. "Look, Nemo, I know you think we're out here in support of some imperialist policy, but I swear to you, AEGIS is a truly international organization. It exists to protect the innocent, free the enslaved, and defend the good in the world from the evil and corruption of the Astrum Argentum."

Doc stepped up beside him, shrugging and smiling. "We really only have a problem with power-hungry fascists and demon-summoning dark magic. Other than that, live and let live."

"Let us help you," Jack urged.

Nemo pursed her lips and nodded. "That is why you are here."

- CHAPTER 18 -

Rivets blinked his eyes open to a steamy prism of sunlight sparkling through palm leaves above. He soon realized he was flat on his back, and a throbbing pain pulsed through his right bicep and his lower left ribs, around back by his kidneys.

He blinked again and glanced to his right. His upper arm had been bandaged with some kind of homespun cloth, which was now stained with blood from the wound. It appeared he was strapped to a well-constructed travois or sledge of some kind, nestled atop a soft bed of moss in a clearing that resembled a lush, tropical garden. Wild bamboo, tree ferns, and fishtail palms thrust skyward, shading colorful hibiscus and orchids, and the entire area was blanketed in a warm midday mist.

Rivets glanced to his left and startled. Crouched just out of the dappled sunlight was what appeared to be a black leopard, some kind of jungle panther, its aquamarine eyes almost aglow in the shadows. When it saw he was conscious, it began to move toward him. Slowly and tentatively at first, then impelled out of curiosity. It wasn't until the large feline form had moved into the light that Rivets realized it wasn't a panther at all, but a human—female—with panther-like features.

Neela slowly looked Rivets over, taking in his scent as well as his form. He was broad around the middle, like Nariaal, and he had the salt-and-pepper whiskers of the Sayer of the Law. She could smell the odor of the invaders from the sky on him, but for some reason she didn't think he belonged to them.

"Where...where are we?" Rivets stammered dryly.

He spoke a peculiar dialect, but Neela understood it as her own language. She wrinkled her nose and whispered, "Safe."

Rivets found himself doing a double-take. The panther-thing could speak, apparently. "I was...I was escaping...I was shot?"

Neela reached into the brush next to the travois and produced the MP-18 Rivets had grabbed from the commando on the beach, which in turn produced a desperate fear reaction in Rivets.

"Whoa, whoa!" he protested, presuming the worst.

Neela saw the anxiety the object created in the stranger, and she immediately put the submachine gun down where she'd found it. "Not to fear," she assured in a soft purr. "The soldiers shot you. I took bullets out, cleaned wounds, bandaged you. You will heal." She looked toward the MP-18 in the underbrush and shrugged. "We know of guns. Nemo uses them to defend us. But we know not of their use."

"If it's all the same to you," Rivets grunted, trying to haul himself upright and failing horribly in the attempt, "just leave the shootin' to me."

The two stared at each other for an awkward minute, before the panther woman broke the silence. "I am Neela," she offered, pointing at her chest with a clawed index finger.

Rivets realized he was the uncivilized one in this group. "Carl," he said sheepishly. "But I go by Rivets."

Neela broke a smile and a laugh escaped her throat. "That is a frog sound."

"Huh? Oh, yeah. Right. Well, it's just a call sign. It's 'cause I build and repair things."

Neela stared at him, unimpressed.

Another silence followed, but this time it was Rivets who spoke first. "So, uh, what... can I ask, that is, what...um, what are you?"

"We are beast folk, the children of Sanctuary," she explained, and Rivets left it at that.

Neela scanned around the clearing periodically, testing the air with her mouth propped slightly open and her tongue pressed against her lower teeth, engaging all her olfactory senses. She was clearly on alert, but didn't seem anxious.

Rivets squirmed on the travois, back and arm throbbing. He tilted his bandaged shoulder toward a pollen-dusted beam of sunlight, examining the dressing. "Did you do this?"

Neela nodded. "I am trained...by Nariaal."

"What's a *narr-ee-all*?"

"He is our wisest. He guides even the Sayer of the Law."

Rivets followed along as best he could, but his mind was still slow and addled. "Sayer of the Law. Right. Right. Well, thank you...for tending my wounds. It's...Neela, right?"

"It is our way," said the panther-woman. "Can you walk? The soldiers are still looking for you, and we still have a long journey to Fort Sanctuary. I cannot pull the travois all that way."

Rivets hoisted himself up to a squatting position. "I think so. Might need to find some kind of walking stick, just so I don't fall down on the trail."

Neela was instantly at Rivets' side, pulling him to his feet and bracing his right arm around her shoulder. "Do not bother with such things," she said. "Lean on me. We will be faster without it."

Rivets winced in pain and fatigue, stumbling to stay upright. He glanced down at the black-furred feline woman bracing his side, and noticed she was waiting for him to signal readiness. He nodded. Then they were gone, disappearing into the misty green jungle, leaving only the makeshift stretcher and some shallow footprints in the mossy clearing.

Maria Blutig exited the gyro-skiff and stormed across the beach, riding crop tucked severely under her arm in a formal manner. Soldiers cleared out of her way as if repelled by a negatively-charged magnet. In the chaos of Holloway's escape, the Silver Star forces had to put down all but two Kanak prisoners. One of the native men had disappeared into the surf, not to be found. For all their trouble, they'd succeeded in trapping only two demons in the infernal engines. Two!

While Himmler was pleased with the overall result, there was no doubt that the process left much room for improvement. But now they were out of sacrifices. She'd already dispatched two commando units to the island's interior to locate and secure more hostages for the ritual, which could continue as soon as they had something to feed the demons summoned from beyond the earthly plane.

Maria was not to stay angry for long. Standing on the beach near the stockade pen was Captain Hummel, looking at a group of prisoners within. Seeing her approach, he offered a smile and a courteous half-bow. "Ah, you got my message," he said. "I brought you a gift."

Maria stood outside the stockade wall and peered through the spaces between the logs. Inside, several pairs of glossy, dark eyes stared back at her. "How many?" she asked, the delight beginning to show on her face.

"Twenty," said Hummel. "And you should see them."

Maria paused. "See them? Are they not Kanak people? How are the different?"

"Oh, my dear," Hummel raised an eyebrow. "The stories of this island are completely true."

He waved a soldier over to the door and told him to open the pen.

What Maria hadn't been able to see through the log spaces was more evident in the sunlight. Feral snouts and ears, shaggy fur and sharp claws, reflective eyes aglow with animal intensity. A sudden wave of relief washed over her.

"How many?" she asked.

"Twenty, including a high value individual, something of a shaman in their society."

Maria nodded, staring into the pen at the creatures arrayed inside. So these were the legendary beast folk of Noble's Isle. Descendants of Moreau's fever dream creations. If she planned this right, she could knock out ten more infernal devices—twenty if she only used a single sacrifice for each summoning—in a session. It would be an exhausting enterprise, but she was willing to push through for the project's sake, and once again bask in Crowley's affection.

Yes, that was it. One sacrifice per summoning. The only reason for two had been to keep the summoned demon slow and sluggish. If Himmler was quick on the trap, they need not worry about the demon escaping. And when they'd filled every last machine, Maria fancied taking one of the local beast folk back to Europe to show Crowley. Perhaps the young ape boy, hiding at the back, behind the older, gray-muzzled feline man.

Nodding at the soldier to close and lock the pen, Maria turned to walk, Hummel joining her in stride.

"I thought you would like them," he said.

"You have quite possibly saved this project, *Mein Kapitän*. I will see to it *Herr* Crowley is informed of your extra diligence."

Hummel smiled inwardly. He knew better than to completely throw his lot in with Maria's. Her relationship with Crowley had been long and productive, but also problematic at times. Crowley had already been informed of the capture of the beast folk courtesy of the radioman on the *Osiris*. Nevertheless, he made a show of deferring to her authority. "Thank you, *meine Führerin*," he said. "I have three units of troops searching for more, and the east side of the island is secure against attack or reprisal."

Maria stopped, lost in thought. She glanced at Hummel with a wicked smile. "*Kapitän,* I wonder if you would loan me two units of commandos for the night? For extra security."

"Extra security?" Hummel quizzed. "For what reason?"

Maria's face went dark with intent. "We continue the ritual tonight."

❧

"What assets do we have on our side?" Jack asked rhetorically, pacing the floor in front of the chart table in Nemo's great hall. "Two lightly-armed airships, twelve aeronauts. One formidable submarine with nothing in the water to destroy..."

Nemo entertained a moment of personal offense before realizing the American pilot was right. This would likely be a conflict which played out on both land and air. She pursed her lips in thought. "We have a heavy machine gun on the aft top deck for shore support. And aside from the crew, *Nautilus* can carry another twenty passengers comfortably."

"What about uncomfortably?" Doc asked.

"Probably forty, with a skeleton crew."

"Good," Jack nodded. "How many fighters can you muster?"

"We have at least fifty among our number here on Tabor Island."

"Range of experience? Any leaders?"

"A wide range, from the Great War to any number of tribal rebellions. There isn't one I wouldn't trust with my life."

Jack looked over Nemo's chart of Sanctuary Island, tracing various entry vectors and scribbling notes in red wax pencil. "It looks like there might be a deep water approach up here, toward the north end."

Nemo nodded. "That is usually where we meet with the local Kanak for news and occasional provisioning. We could send a small force in inflatable boats to the island."

"I'll volunteer," said Deadeye, stepping forward.

Kate Shakespeare's brown eyes gleamed from under the bangs of her auburn bob cut. "And I."

Jack arched an eyebrow and traded looks between the two of them. "You're both experienced guerrilla fighters," he acknowledged. "But with both of you on the island, we won't have anyone in the airship turrets."

"If I may," Nemo suggested, leaned forward onto the chart table, "I can ask for volunteers from our island defense personnel to replace your turret gunners."

Jack and Doc exchanged a glance with Duke, who nodded in agreement.

"That's just fine," Jack said. He focused his attention back on the chart. "If we send two small units ashore on the north side, they'll be able to reach Fort Sanctuary from a rear approach, and reinforce the beast folk."

"The beast folk of Sanctuary are my charges," Nemo stated firmly. "I would rather they not have to take up arms, though I realize that particular horse has already left the barn by now. Nonetheless, I will also lead a unit ashore, so there will be three."

"That still leaves us a bit thin up top," Duke remarked.

"Duke brings up a good point," Jack said. "While we've never been in position to face either of those ships in open combat, we still need to split the Silver Star's forces as much as possible."

"The more fighters are engaged with us," Duke said, "the fewer are strafing our ground force."

"Those carriers are real monsters," Jack explained. "The *Luftpanzer* has a battery of artillery guns on each side, and carries three fighters for support and reconnaissance. We've never come close enough to the *Osiris* to see what it's packing for firepower, but it carries six fighters."

"Six fighters," Duke repeated, the wheels in his mind already spinning.

Doc knew immediately what he was thinking about. "The gyro-packs?"

Jack's eyes widened. "Of course!"

Nemo squinted. "Gyro-packs?"

Jack's grin was ear-to-ear as he jawed a stick of gum. "Each of our airships carries three gyro-packs. They're like a personal gyro-copter with a couple Tommy guns for defense. They're light and maneuverable, they pack a decent punch, and make a smaller target than a plane or an airship." He leaned over the table and winked at Nemo. "Doc and I have used them to fight pterodactyls over the Congo."

Nemo looked skeptical. "Pterodactyls?"

"Hey," Jack countered, "you have a mino-taur." He saluted the ox-headed crewman with a wink.

"Thing is," Doc warned, "they're not easy to fly. We'd need trained pilots to wear them, which would leave our airships without a helm."

Jack took Duke's arm and walked him to a corner of the great hall, away from the main crowd. All eyes followed. They conversed back and forth for a brief moment before returning to the chart table. Jack slapped both palms on the table surface.

"We're going to consolidate crews," Jack announced. *Daedalus* will take point in this fight. *Percival* will remain here on Tabor Island. Duke, Doc, myself, Cipher, and Asim will take five of the gyro-packs. Barrett will pilot the *Daedalus,* and Nemo will assign a naviga-tor, radio operator, and two gunners."

Barrett, with her sandy hair tucked into a khaki bush hat, cracked a smile. So far, AEGIS service had not been boring.

Jack continued. "Duke, Cipher, and Asim will run interference with the fighter planes, and Doc and I will try to get onto the *Luftpanzer* and rescue Rivets...maybe indulge in a little sabotage while we're up there."

Doc nodded. "We do have those captured Silver Star uniforms."

"If the carriers are anchored," Barrett drawled in her Aussie accent, "we can come in high enough for you to drop down in the gyro-packs without raising too much fuss."

"And even if the Silver Star did have our radio detection technology," Cipher mentioned, "and I don't think they do...the gyro-packs wouldn't make much of a blip."

"So it's a plan," Jack said, pointing at various positions on the chart. "Three shore parties, two gyro units, *Nautilus* for sea-based support, and the *Daedalus* for aerial support. The objective is to save native lives and kick the Silver Star off Sanctuary Island, recover the stolen dynamo—if it still exists—and retrieve Commander Holloway if he's alive."

"From a strictly pragmatic standpoint, what happens if we lose this fight?" Nemo asked.

"Then evil will have its day," Jack answered without a trace of sarcasm. "And I'm not willing to let that be the outcome."

- CHAPTER 19 -

With the moon a mere sliver waxing white in the star-strewn sky over the Pacific, Maria Blutig gathered her acolytes and soldiers on the western beach head, and once again proceeded to tear open the membrane between dimensions. Torches and braziers flickered with amber firelight, casting strange shadows across the white sand and the sun-bleached palm logs of the picket wall. Hummel's additional forces stood at the ready.

The Sayer of the Law was hauled into the sacrificial cage atop the altar, and the chanting began.

Maria stood in the protective cone under the altar, raising her palms upward. "Elder gods of the dark universe before and after time, I call upon thee! Denizens of the eldritch dimension *Narakam*, hear me. Feel my power and take heed. I summon a single demon-form of the *shayatin*—come forth into this world and feed!"

Again, the cultists chanted: *Shayatin, shayatin, come forth and feed!*

A distant roll of thunder—rather, what sounded distant but actually had erupted from the local area above the altar—crackled and pulsed as the space around the sound began to warp, an unseen, alien force flexing at the veil.

Once again, a bespectacled Himmler stood at the ready, his hands on the trap controls.

Shayatin, shayatin, come forth and feed!

Gradually, the wound in the flesh between dimensions tore open, and the spindly, clawed legs emerged from the localized tempest. Within moments, the entire body—part arachnoid, part piscine, part something ancient and horrible—dropped onto the altar. It immediately fixed on the Sayer of the Law, held within the wooden prison cell. Multiple eyes regarded the sacrifice momentarily.

But instead of feeding, it leaped toward the picket wall like a giant flea.

The troops stationed around the beach turned and exchanged looks, unsure of the best course of action as the entity took two leaps, clearing the barrier. Within seconds, it had vanished in the jungle.

Maria and the cultists continued their chanting, as yet unaware of the entity's disappearance.

The rift remained open.

Another set of claw-tipped legs reached through.

The pristine, mirror-like surface of the Pacific began to roil and bubble, and the conning tower and top deck of the *Nautilus* broke the surface a hundred yards from shore. Hatches were immediately thrown open and crew began to emerge, scurrying about various tasks. Three rubberized canvas pontoon boats were unrolled on the afterdeck and inflated with compressed air. Short paddles were distributed among the crew.

Deadeye wore his Winchester repeater on his back inside a waterproof sheath of a similar material as the boats. He climbed into the first boat, along with five of Nemo's hand-picked marines. Four were of Indian extraction, while the fifth was the large bovine-headed fellow who had welcomed Jack and Cipher aboard the *Nautilus* not long ago. Deadeye watched as the other two boats filled quickly: Nemo took the centermost, with her Chinese bosun, three Indian sailors, and a hyena-woman who knew the island like the back of her fur-covered hand. Kate Shakespeare headed the leftmost boat, filled out with four Indian sailors and a canine-man whose senses would benefit their tracking efforts. The dog-man's elongated muzzle and large, arrow-head ears cut a very "Egyptian god" figure, and Deadeye couldn't help but marvel that they had both Anubis and the legendary minotaur with their little army.

Nemo's boat pushed away from the after-deck first, taking point as the others followed in a triangular formation toward the sundered dock. They paddled almost silently through the dark night, leaving scant ripples in their wake.

Once the flat bottoms of the boats began to drag on the sand, the crews jumped out and hauled their craft up onto the beach, piling the paddles within. The village they found was a burned-out husk. Nothing was left alive, and the dead still lay where they'd fallen days ago.

Out of habit, Deadeye knelt in the cover of what had been a hut, shrugging the rifle from his shoulder and removing it from its sheath. He glanced to his right and saw Kate was doing the same with her Lee-Enfield. Although

Deadeye was used to scouting ahead, planting ambushes and taking point in general, Nemo and her people knew this island far better than he, so he deferred and instructed his group to follow Nemo's as they took the main trail into the jungle.

The AEGIS field agents had expected the *Nautilus* compliment to be armed with a variety of military surplus, but every crew member carried a hand-built gyrojet weapon. This gun used an unknown chemical which super-heated on ignition, propelling the projectile for a longer burn than standard gunpowder. The weapon was most effective underwater, but could be fired on land, as well.

Despite the lack of moonlight, a dazzling array of constellations provided a modicum of illumination to navigate by. They would hug the west coast of the island, negotiating around the more mountainous interior terrain. Fort Sanctuary lay a mile from a large inlet on the northwest side, a hard journey of almost seven miles at a fast march. Between the northwestern inlet and a second one to the southwest lay a square-ish peninsula, on the outer shore of which stood Maria Blutig's fortified beach head. Due to the presence of a magnificent volcanic mountain covered in thick vegetation sitting squarely in the middle of the peninsula, the Silver Star had remained initially unaware of their proximity to both

Fort Sanctuary and the House of Pain. However, since their initial invasion, there were now Silver Star soldiers spread throughout the island, in the jungles, and across the mountain plateaus.

They'd gone perhaps three miles when Nemo's hyena-woman stopped short, raising her fist,signaling the others to halt. Deadeye immediately felt every hair on his neck and arms perk up. She'd obviously picked up a scent.

A single *crack!* rang out, and the hyena-woman's head parted with the force of the rifle shot. She dropped instantly.

Deadeye clenched his jaw and flagged his troops to find cover and stay put. As he'd feared, there was a sniper about. His unit scampered into crouched or prone positions in the cover of some split-leaf palms, and he rolled away from the path into some under-brush near Nemo. "Stay down," he told her, waving for Kate to crawl forward. "I'm gonna draw his fire. Watch for the muzzle flash and see if you can take him out."

"Roger that," she replied softly in her British accent. Wetting her thumb on her tongue, she moistened the sights on the Lee-Enfield and put the rifle to her cheek.

Deadeye wriggled on his belly across the sandy, root-veined soil to a low vantage behind a pumice formation. He wasn't sure which tree was providing the sniper's nest, but had narrowed his best guess to three coconut palms on the rise above the trail. Racking the lever on the Winchester, he split the difference and fired at the center tree, ducking down immediately. Bark and pulp exploded from the bullet's impact, and an instant reprisal exploded from the third palm, kicking a chunk of lava rock over Deadeye's head. Less than a second later, a third shot rang out from the bushes on the other side of the trail. An injured cry erupted from the dark of the trees, and a body fell from its nest, landing in the trail with a hollow *thud*.

Nemo rose and led her contingent to the sniper's corpse, which was already beginning to sizzle and smoke. Despite the low light, Deadeye could see the look of shock on her face as he passed.

"Best leave it," he warned. "They do that."

"All the time?" Nemo found herself wondering aloud.

"All the time," answered Kate as she ejected the spent shell casing from her rifle and slapped the bolt back down.

Nemo watched the sniper dissolve into a pile of ash and bone fragments under a tent of gray fatigues. Though she was usually unflappable in tense battle situations, this rattled her. As she waved her troops onward to follow Deadeye's unit, she acknowledged that they were dealing with a very different kind of enemy.

ଔ

The *Daedalus* came in over the island at ten thousand feet, with no running lights to give them away. Sheila Barrett manned the pilot's seat, Fraser at the nav station, and Farmingham on comms.

In the aft cargo bay, Jack and Doc joined Duke, Cipher, and Asim. Unlike their compatriots, the two were dressed in Silver Star officer uniforms, accurate down to the collar tabs and spit-shined jackboots. Their officers' caps were stowed in a small satchel strapped across each of their bodies, secured at the left hip. Doc's bag also contained a couple of Tesla grenades and basic first aid supplies, while Jack, not content with the 9mm sidearm strapped to his Silver Star officer's belt, stowed the twin Colts in his own satchel.

Each of them donned a pair of flight goggles. They would have no radio contact for this part of the mission. If any of them were shot down and somehow survived, they were to make contact with Nemo's ground force by any means necessary.

Sparks helped each pilot adjust the harness and control arms of the gyro-pack as it was put on, making mental notes of all the improvements she would make to them once the mission was finished.

The gyro-pack itself was about the size of an arctic backpack, with a cylindrical housing behind a padded backrest and a small bicycle saddle. The housing contained a single dynamo generator connected to an electric motor, which drove a pair of balanced rotor blades less than a foot over the pilot's head. Two control armatures folded upward from the spine, with simple pitch and yaw joysticks atop each. The right stick also twisted to control throttle, which was an odd revelation to pilots without experience riding motorcycles. Each stick also sported a thumb trigger for the modified Thompson SMG under each arm, and the guns had the stocks removed so they consisted only of the chamber, barrel and a sixty-round drum magazine. Although light by cargo standards, the whole assembly weighed close to eighty pounds. It was an elegant conveyance in the air, but extremely awkward during takeoff and landing.

Duke fastened a leather flight helmet under his chin, adjusting his goggles. "Haven't flown these in a year or so," he chimed. "And pterodactyls don't generally shoot back."

Jack smiled, patting Duke on the cheek. "You'll be fine, old man." He turned to Cipher, who had swapped her ubiquitous service beret for a flight cap identical to Duke's. "You okay, Cipher?" he asked.

"Not really," she answered honestly. "But standing around here with eighty pounds of gear on my back isn't going to change that."

Jack laughed at her candor. "That's the spirit."

Doc caught sight of Asim, who looked positively ghostly with fear. She went to help tighten his harness and squeeze his shoulder, which felt like an iron bar. His hands were shaking.

"Just follow Duke and Cipher," she said earnestly. "You'll be just fine, Ace."

Asim blinked and cocked his head. Had he heard right? Had Doc just given him a nickname?

"Alright crew," Jack announced, "When Sparks lowers the cargo bay door, we're gonna make our jump. Remember these things only have about a 5,000-foot service ceiling, so once we drop, we're not coming back up the same way. Rendezvous with Nemo and Deadeye on the island. Last one back buys the drinks!"

Sparks hit the red industrial button on the gondola wall, and the aft cargo hatch began to lower on a pair of large hydraulic pistons. Duke stood in the center of the deck until the hatch door lowered far enough to grant clearance for the gyro-pack's four-foot rotors on either side of his head. "Right," he announced over the whistle of wind, "three-count spacing, form up on me at five thousand feet!" He then turned to the open door and fell away into the darkness below. *"Tally ho!"*

Cipher stepped into Duke's place, holding her breath and counting to three. Stepping forward, she let the breeze pull her from the deck plate.

Asim had been fully recharged by the gift of Doc's nickname, though she would never know the full extent. Smiling, he clapped Jack on the shoulder. "She called me Ace! *My nickname is Ace!*" Then he leaped from the open deck and was gone.

Jack and Doc stood together in the cargo bay and exchanged a long look.

"This is crazy!" Jack shouted over the wind.

Doc grinned. "And how, brother! And how!"

"Good luck!" Sparks waved from the door controls. "See you on the ground!"

Jack turned and gave Sparks a two-fingered Boy Scout salute, then grabbed Doc and kissed her as tightly and firmly as he could without entangling their rotor blades. He mouthed the words *I love you,* and folded a stick of Black Jack between his smiling teeth. Three steps later, he was falling feet-first into the air.

His face stung at the chill wind. Despite the tropical locale, it was still night, and he was ten thousand feet in the sky. A sudden worry—or more accurately, a perverse notion—crossed his mind. If the gyro-pack didn't start, he'd have a nice two-mile drop into the ocean. That would be quite an end to a storied career.

Twisting the throttle, he heard the electric motor whine and felt the vibration of the rotors spinning up. He knew they wouldn't be much good except for slowing descent until he made five thousand feet, so he relaxed his legs and made a small circle downward, aiming for the large, well-lit vehicle below: the *Luftpanzer II.* Glancing upward, he could see the small, black gap in the stars in the shape of the *Daedalus'* envelope. He couldn't hear anything aside from the electric motor whirring against his back, but he knew Doc was somewhere right above him.

The battle to rescue his friend...that was below him.

- CHAPTER 20 -

Maria felt something was off. It had been several seconds, and she hadn't sensed the creature feed. What was it doing? "Feed, shay-atan, feed!" she urged from within the protective cone beneath the altar. Looking out past the semicircle of kneeling acolytes, she saw the panicked look on soldiers' faces, and she came to a stark realization.

They were coming through, but they weren't feeding. Perhaps they didn't have a taste for beast folk. For whatever reason, the summoned eldritch terrors were escaping the beach compound to find sustenance else-where.

Suddenly Himmler was blocking the torch-light in the opening of the protective altar frame, waving his hands maniacally. "Stop! You must seal the rift and stop the summoning!"

Maria froze in place, unsure of her next move. Moments later her wits returned and she closed her eyes, chanting at the altar above her head. "*Et oblinito mea essentia mihi et odium, omnem antiquis res est inanis!*" she asserted, thrusting her essence upward to seal the dimensional tear through sheer force of will.

But it was too late. The eldritch terrors continued clawing their way through the fabric of time and space as from an egg sac. Two more spilled out on the altar, while another four sprang toward the picket wall and freedom beyond. Soon the beach head would be overrun.

Maria had no intention of becoming a demon's psychic meal. "*Herr* Himmler!" she barked as the tip of a slender claw hooked under the lip of the casting chamber doorway. "Wire as many traps from the generator as you can! Capture them as they feed, or even on the run. Go!"

The scientist disappeared, shouting orders at his field team.

Focusing her mind and will, Maria breathed deeply, secure in the knowledge that if anyone could turn such a debacle into a victory, it was she.

☙

Duke scanned below as Cipher and Ace formed up on his left and right, respectively. Almost a mile down, brazier fires and electric spotlights illuminated the western beach, and some sort of activity was happening in the Silver Star encampment. The *Luftpanzer* swayed at her mooring cable in the evening breeze. A single fighter escort, a brand new Heinkel HD 23, sat unmanned atop the flat runway spine of the carrier. No other support aircraft could be seen. Just a month ago, the Silver Star were using Fokker C.V.D. fighters. Whether they'd upgraded to the lighter, faster Heinkels out of desire, or due to the fact that Duke and his compatriots had destroyed their entire known compliment of Fokkers over the Eastern Desert of Egypt, was unknown.

Well there's a bit of luck, Duke thought. Leaning forward, he throttled faster on the right joystick and went into a shallow spiral dive, circling over the island. Most everything was a carpet of black jungle and dead volcanic mountaintops, with a few exceptions. A small collection of lights on the eastern shore indicated the second Silver Star camp, but Duke couldn't see where the *Osiris* was tethered. Another bright spot emanated from the north-western inlet a mile from the peninsula. *That must be Fort Sanctuary,* he thought, remembering the map of the island and what Nemo had told them prior to departure.

Hang on, thought Duke as he leaned into a right turn and circled back on his larger arc. Once again he picked out a collection of lights on the eastern shore, the secondary Silver Star camp. There wasn't much beach on that side of the island—on any side, really. Most of the shoreline was rocky and sheer, with only a few small, sandy beaches for easy ingress.

The eastern encampment looked sparse and undermanned.

The *Osiris* was nowhere to be found.

∾

Jack eased slowly off the gyro-pack throttle and came in to land softly on the *Luftpanzer*'s aft deck behind the flight hangar, just right of the massive dorsal tail fin. He wasn't sure if the flight control officer had seen him land, and he wasn't about to ask. Jack immediately shrugged out of the gyro harness and swapped the leather flight cap and goggles with the officer's cap from his satchel. The hangar bay was an elongated box standing on the spine of the giant airship, used for storing and deploying their single-man fighter planes, rather than carrying them under the ship's belly. He couldn't see the status of the front doors and didn't want to risk suspicion by walking in off the runway. He looked around for an alternate entry as Doc came down behind and to his right.

Within seconds, she'd released her own pack and was at Jack's side, straightening her uniform cap. Jack regarded her silently for a moment. Although the Silver Star did include female officers in its ranks, the stolen uniform Doc wore had not been tailored for one. Fortunately all the individual components were the same, so it was merely a case of cinching the belt a bit more and hoping casual observers failed to notice a wider cut to the jodhpurs. The lower left jacket sleeve did appear noticeably bulky in comparison to the right, but Jack knew it was because she was wearing the Athenean vambrace underneath, gifted to her by Marina Stavros. With the protection spell already invoked, Jack was hopeful it could shield them both against incoming fire.

Nodding approval, Jack pointed around the corner to an exterior door hatch. With Doc following closely behind, Jack stealthily strode to the door and hauled the locking mechanism to the open position, swinging it open. He paused a moment, then stepped inside, followed by Doc.

The hangar bay was a large, rectangular garage space, lined with racks of mechanics' tools and a small crane for moving airplane engines. Jack noted the floor was painted with delineations for where planes were to be parked and cleated down for transport. The room was devoid of aircraft; only the single fighter on the outer tarmac was anywhere in the vicinity. It looked like the *Luftpanzer II* carried a compliment of three fighters. He marveled at what the flight deck of the *Osiris* must look like, as it carried twice as many.

Fortunately, the deck officer was on the other side of the hangar and hadn't seen Lieutenants Botin and Ludwig enter through the maintenance hatch. Nor would he have known that Lieutenants Botin and Ludwig had both been assigned to the Athens garrison six months ago, and had died at the hands of AEGIS field agents within the previous month.

Jack and Doc made their way to the main stairwell down at a businesslike pace—not so fast as to attract attention, yet not so slow as to look like they didn't know where they were going. The deck officer gave a cursory salute from the far side of the hangar, and Jack returned the gesture.

Although Jack and Doc both knew some German, neither had used it actively in some time, so they were both gratified to see signage posted in both German and English. Two decks down was the first of two main decks, containing facilities like the brig, interrogation rooms, and one of two radio rooms. Jack stepped onto the central gantry and waved Doc forward. "Security," he nodded at the sign on the interior wall. "Let see if we can find Rivets."

With her right hand resting on the holstered pistol at her hip, yet trying to look casual, Doc led the way down the hall. They passed access panels and air vents, ductwork and bundled cabling. Making their way forward, they finally came across the brig. As Jack tried the door handle, only to find it locked, a Silver Star soldier—an ensign by the look of his shoulder—turned down the hallway from a side chamber, hailing the two of them.

"*Was kann ich Ihnen helfen, meine Offiziere?*"

Jack felt a brief flush of panic rise in his throat, but Doc blurted out, "*Gefangenentransfer.*"

Prisoner transfer? Jack thought. *Not a bad story. I'd believe her.*

The young ensign nodded in understanding, and Jack was almost convinced they might get his assistance in unlocking the door. Then the ensign squinted and Jack suddenly realized he was still jawing that stick of chewing gum from the drop. Between the faint licorice odor wafting from his mouth and the obvious gum-chewing action, Jack realized they'd been made.

Or had they?

In an act of undercover desperation, Jack reached into the belt satchel and produced a pack of Black Jack. He fished a stick up from the pack and offered it to the ensign, whose demeanor shifted immediately. A senior officer who was bucking the rules had offered this younger man a courtesy. Smiling, the ensign plucked the stick of gum from the pack and unwrapped it. Instantly, Jack's right fist rocketed forward, flattening the officer's nose in a scarlet explosion. The young man fell back against the interior wall, and Doc had his keys within seconds. Jack leaned against the man, holding his unconscious body upright.

Doc fished a small selection of keys to find the one that opened the main brig door. Jack pulled the ensign inside behind her. The room was quite dark, save for some basic emergency lighting. A row of cells stood against the outer wall, completely lined with bars.

In the leftmost cell was a cot with a worn mattress, soaked through with blood. A gray mechanic's cap lay crumpled in the corner. Doc stifled a cry, and Jack saw it immediately. Rivets had been held here. But what had they done with him?

"What now?" Doc asked.

Jack drummed his fingers on the Silver Star belt around his waist. "Part of me wants to toss those Tesla grenades into the ballonets and get out of here, but another part really wants answers."

"There's also the dynamo," she reminded him.

"That too, if the *'kaput'* message was malarkey," he agreed. "Let's get to the bridge, see if we can get someone to tell us what's going on."

℞

Nemo's group broke out of the jungle a hundred yards shy of the twenty-foot-high white stone walls of Fort Sanctuary. She pulled a small flare gun from her inside breast pocket and fired a red comet into the air.

Immediately, the giant fifteen-foot wooden gates swung open, and the ground contingent was met by a few dozen beast folk of all varieties. A jaguar woman stood next to a muscular man with a porcine face. A couple peered their canine heads from behind the crowd. A water buffalo man with gray hair and milky eyes wore the raiment of an elder. Standing in the center of the welcoming crowd of animal hybrids was a great silverback gorilla, a hewn quarterstaff in his hand. Clutching his waist was a smaller male gorilla in a flaxen shirt and pants.

Nemo strode forward, happy to see her old friend. At least, that's what it appeared to Deadeye, who kept one eye on the fort and another on his and Kate's contingent. The giant ape padded forward on deceptively silent feet, finally stopping to allow her to complete the distance.

"Thank you for answering my call, Nemo," the ape said.

Nemo wrapped him in an embrace that dwarfed her. "My good friend Nariaal," she said. "I only wish I could have come sooner. I brought some help."

"Well son-of-a-gun," came a Bronx-tinged growl from the crowd. Deadeye looked up to see a smiling Carl Holloway, limping, bruised and hatless, stalking toward him.

"I don't believe it," Deadeye chuckled, shaking his head as he went in for a bear hug. "We thought the Silver Star had gotten tired of your war stories and shot you."

Rivets laughed. "Ha! Well, they did shoot me," he said, pointing at his shoulder. "But that was for escaping before dinner time." He was gaunt and considerably more slender than any time Deadeye could remember. Even during the worst of the Great War, Rivets had been a fireplug. But now his ripped and ratty coveralls hung off him, his once majestic mustache drooping sadly like the whiskers of an old walrus.

Deadeye couldn't help but notice the feral look from the eyes of the panther-woman standing next to Rivets. The older mechanic saw his glance and introduced her.

"Uh, this is Neela. She saved my life."

Deadeye smiled broadly. "AEGIS owes you a drink, miss."

Smiling awkwardly, Neela was unsure what the comment meant, but the inference was positive.

Nariaal waved the incoming soldiers into the safety of the fort, where they gathered in the flickering light of torches and lanterns. Multi-level homes of bamboo and stone crowded around a central square, with dirt path tendrils extending away into the village. "Your friend Rivets has informed us what is happening on the western beach," the ape-man rumbled. "They are opening a rift to summon demons that they entrap to use as a power source."

"Unbelievable," Nemo cried, shocked.

Deadeye shook his head again. "Not really," he said. "This is kind of their game. Question is, what are we doing about it?"

"I will join any force going to drive the invaders from our shores," Nariaal announced. "Until then, the prohibition on spilling blood is suspended. We must protect our home."

Deadeye could only imagine the experience of running into battle next to a gorilla. He snapped his fingers at someone back in the ranks who came forward clutching one of Nemo's gyrojet guns in his hands. But Deadeye wanted what the sailor had slung over his shoulder. Taking the MP-18 from the sailor, he handed it to Nariaal.

The great ape was familiar with the history of this island, and he'd read a lot of books on various subjects. There wasn't a topic he couldn't regurgitate some random facts about. He knew about wars and he knew about much of the technology used to wage them. But he'd never fired a gun. Nariaal grabbed the stock of the submachine gun and hefted its weight instinctively. Then he locked eyes with Deadeye. "Show me."

- CHAPTER 21 -

Jack and Doc descended another stairwell and found themselves on the lower main gantry that ran the length of the carrier. So far they had only encountered three Silver Star personnel, and not aroused any suspicion. Except perhaps for the young ensign who was currently bound and gagged, locked inside Rivets' old cell on the security level.

Jack looked both ways to get his bearings. Forward lay the bridge, aft the drive systems. The twin lift envelopes ran parallel to the central gantry on either side. The *Luftpanzer* had an enormous ballonet chamber on either side, each container filled with combustible hydrogen. It gave Jack an idea. As much as he wanted to get to the bridge, this was too good an opportunity to let pass.

"Change of plans. Come with me, Doc," he said, moving aft. "We'll need those Tesla grenades."

Doc pulled on his arm to stop him in his tracks. "Why don't I give you the grenades and I can check out the bridge? I have the vambrace for protection."

Jack sighed. "Haven't we worked together long enough to grasp the virtues of the Buddy System?" He pulled back, taking her with him. "I'm not leaving you, and you're not leaving me."

She couldn't very well argue against the Buddy System. It was drummed into every operative in AEGIS field training, along with Rule #1: Never split up the party—which they ended up doing all the time. Of course there would be situations where Rule #1 could not or would not apply, therefore the absolute focus on the Buddy System.

Doc wrenched her hand back. "Okay, okay. Buddy System. Jeez."

They hit a cross-platform amidships, and Jack knew either of the passages led to the topmost access to the envelopes. He chose starboard at random. They passed ranks of crew quarters before the passage terminated at a hatch door. While Doc kept watch, Jack levered the handle and pulled the door open, stepping through onto a perforated aluminum catwalk running fore and aft. To the outside of the catwalk was a vulcanized canvas wall, labeled in sections.

Perfect.

"Hey, Doc," he whisper-shouted back into the passage. "Toss me that bag, will ya?"

Doc shrugged the satchel from her shoulder and and threw it through the doorway to Jack.

He caught it, and, reaching inside, found one of the fist-sized cylinders within. Flicking open the safety catch on the outer housing, he released the generator core, which popped up about two inches from the center of the device. A phosphorescent marker on the face of the core shone against a series of hash marks in a circle around it on the housing, divided by fives, each representing a minute. He turned the core to the twenty-minute mark and pressed it back in, arming the grenade.

Jack stowed the device back in the satchel, which he shoved through the seam between two canvas panels. He felt the bag come to rest atop another rubberized canvas bag, which he could tell by its shape was an actual hydrogen ballonet.

Doc braced herself in the passage as she heard a couple of crewmen walking aft. The passed the cross-platform without noticing her at the far end. She exhaled silently. Suddenly Jack was behind her, levering the hatch shut.

"We're in business," he said. "Twenty minutes."

❧

Himmler's team resembled a wild gymnastics troupe in the midst of No Man's Land on the Western Front. They ran to and fro on the pale sand in the almost-moonless night, stringing wires to electronic traps and setting them out under ravening extradimensional demons. Himmler himself threw every switch while dodging panicked soldiers.

The commandos ran for whatever cover they could manage on the flat sand, only to be eaten alive by the pouncing predators. Bodies and body parts littered the beach.

One of Himmler's technicians made the mistake of looking into the four glassy spider eyes of one of the eldritch horrors, freezing in place as his essence was siphoned away. For a moment of terror, the technician felt himself bonded with the alien psyche, as agonizing as any vision of hell. Then his body dropped, a dry, empty husk. The creature sank low on its spindly, clawed legs, bloated and sluggish.

Himmler was sorry to lose Karl, but he flipped the switch that activated the trap, imprisoning the thing that had devoured his friend. That machine would go on to power an army.

Sometimes they got lucky and trapped one before it had fed. Occasionally, a technician would have to approach a soldier in the process of being impaled on razor-sharp claws while his soul was ripped away, tossing the wired trap at the feet of the assaulting demon. One thing became clear very quickly: when a demon fed, it didn't move—it was completely focused on the absorption of its psychic food.

If the beach outside the altar was chaos, the space within the protective cone was quiet and serene as Maria Blutig scanned her memories for an invocation that would repair the rift just ten feet above her head. She had a brief moment of panic when nothing came. Then she recalled a lecture that her mentor Crowley had given in Paris, about the power of pure will.

She glanced down at the acolytes kneeling at her feet. Selecting a pretty young girl in the front, she extended a slender, pale hand. "Rise, child."

The young woman stood, crimson robes hanging from her lithe form.

"Come here," Maria ordered, and the woman obeyed.

Maria placed her hands at the woman's temples, caressing the blonde hair pinned back under the gown's hood. The woman opened her eyes and locked them with Maria's intent gaze.

"Yield to me," she whispered, "and live forever."

Without awaiting an answer, Maria opened the channel to siphon the acolyte's life force from her young body. The young woman tried to scream, but the sound that erupted from her throat was the unholy groan of torment of a soul ripped from its earthly body. This was exactly what the summoned demons did to feed, and it was usually something Maria only did to replenish her strength after a difficult spell casting. But for the task at hand, she needed that extra signal boost, that little pop to put her over the bar.

The acolyte shriveled and fell away into a dry heap the consistency of raked fall leaves. As the soft ocean breeze began to blow bits of her ash across the threshold of the casting chamber, the other acolytes looked up and ceased their chanting. A horde of unspeakable eldritch demons crouched on the altar above them, gazing down on the kneeling figures with those black spider eyes, clicking their talons on the wooden frame.

One of the remaining acolytes turned and rose to escape, only to be torn limb from limb as one of the entities sprang on him, crimson robes soaked in a darker hue.

Acolytes were ripped apart one by one, screaming their death throes to an uncaring universe as terrors from another dimension feasted on their anguish and life essence. One by one, the demons were sucked into Himmler's electric machines, stacked on the beach near the gyro skiff.

A soft grumble of thunder rolled across the beach, which was now laden in a shallow mist. The last of the traps was activated, its target ensnared. One last entity sprang toward the picket wall and was shredded by machine gun fire from the sentry on the battlement.

Himmler looked at the carnage strewn across the beach. He'd filled close to fifty infernal machines, and there were perhaps ten soldiers remaining. All of the occultist acolytes had been killed. He glanced inside the casting chamber, and swallowed dryly.

The sky above the altar was still and silent. Maria had disappeared.

❧

Duke was circling on his second pass over the island when he heard it: the telltale whine of a Heinkel fighter. The bastards had been out here all the time, but were returning from a much higher search vector. Now they'd get into the scrap.

By instinct, he angled down into a corkscrew dive, skirting the jungle canopy between the fern-covered peaks of extinct volcanoes.

Cipher saw the action and followed, leaving Ace hovering above them.

The first tracer round blazed green just inches past Ace's head. Momentarily panicked, he cranked hard on the throttle and leaned back in an effort to see where the attack had come from. This angled the rotors backward at a great burst of speed, sending him up and over in an inverted loop. As he arced over, the top silhouette of the fighter loomed up at him. Without thinking, both joystick triggers were squeezed, sending a hail of tracerless 45-caliber ammunition down into the single pilot's compartment, tearing through the Silver Star soldier at the stick. The Heinkel immediately dipped and fell toward the jungle, leaving Ace breathing in gulps as he stabilized his flight path and joined the others.

"Watch your fire!" Duke called out as the others formed up on him. "They're coming in after us! Stay close to the canopy in case you take a hit!"

As expected, the initial fighter had been the lead plane, and his wingmen were not far behind. Both sprayed green fire across the island and into the jungle below. Cipher was the first to peel off to the left, and Ace followed her action in reverse, angling right.

The first fighter took Cipher's bait, rolling to the left in pursuit.

The second pilot glanced over her shoulder to see if she could tell what Ace's approximate vector would be, then throttled forward on Duke, machine gun blazing in green ribbons of light.

Duke pitched to the right and leaned backward, arcing up in a slow somersault. As he passed the zenith and felt the momentary lapse of gravity, he caught the front silhouette of the plane as it flashed green with every tracer shot from the guns. Hitting both Thompson triggers, he unleashed a staccato assault, tearing chunks out of the Heinkel's propeller and sparking an engine fire.

The pilot cursed as she angled away from the island toward a crash landing in the water.

Cipher banked and swerved, but the fighter plane was too fast and maneuverable. Her only advantage was that she provided a small target, and an almost invisible one at that. It was all she could do to evade the stream of glowing green death edging closer and closer with every burst.

She felt an explosion of pain from her lower extremities, and looked down to see her left calf had been shot through. Though she couldn't see most of the damage, a stabbing, throbbing ache flooded her whole leg. Cipher knew she was loosing blood. She was almost sorry it hadn't been a tracer round, as the burning barium salts might have at least cauterized the wound as the round penetrated.

As it was, she wouldn't be able to stay aloft much longer. She banked hard to the right and headed toward Fort Sanctuary as fast as the battery could turn the gyro blades. The Heinkel turned with her and continued firing.

Ace dropped down behind the plane, shooting up its tail assembly while Duke blasted the pilot's compartment from the side. The reinforced fuselage repelled or absorbed much of the damage, but a few rounds made it over the top and tore into the pilot's face, killing him. The plane dropped into the jungle, and the three gyro-packs formed up together.

Suddenly the air was full of green and red tracers, the island canopy blinking like Christmas lights. The other squadron of fighters was barreling in fast—and the *Daedalus* was in the middle of the swarm.

☙

"Twenty minutes?!" Doc stammered, certain she'd not heard Jack correctly.

Jack pulled one of the nickel-plated Colts from his satchel and racked the slider to check inside. "Uh huh," he muttered, scanning down the corridor. "Let's go."

As he set foot on the main gantry and proceeded forward, Doc pressed him for details.

"Just what do you hope to accomplish in twenty minutes?"

"This is the first time you've complained to me about it," Jack winked. As he glanced back at Doc, who rolled her eyes at the ribald reference, he caught some motion down the aft corridor and turned to bolt, unconsciously taking Doc's hand as he ran. "That vambrace spell of yours still up?" he asked as they pressed forward.

"Far as I know," said Doc, finally pulling her hand back. "Bridge," she pointed.

The door hatch was the same as every other on the ship: aluminum plating with a deadbolt lever that kept it shut when necessary. Jack shifted the lever and swung open the hatch.

They stepped onto a raised platform that overlooked the entire bridge. It was an enormous affair, more comparable to a large oceangoing vessel than an aircraft, down to the twin steering wheels and ratcheting engine speed indicator. Doc pulled the hatch closed behind them and locked the lever.

A woman stood over a table of navigational charts, while a young man sat at a complex radio listening station. Neither steering wheel was manned, although a handful of officers stood about on the lower deck and chatting in private conversation. The older gentleman near the main windscreen array was someone Jack recognized. Captain Jonas Ecke, terror of London during the war, now looking nothing but dignified in his black uniform and cap with red piping.

The security guard posted on the inside of the hatch tried to unholster his Luger, but Jack grabbed it with his left hand, pulled it from the holster, and pistol whipped the officer, who fell unconscious to the floor.

All eyes shot to the upper bridge deck.

"Ah," said Jack, sticking the pistol in his belt and raising his own .45 in the air. "Good. I have your attention."

The elderly captain with the white fisherman's beard stepped forward. "*Kapitän* Stratosphere," he marveled. "I did not expect to see you again so soon."

"Captain Ecke," Jack nodded. "We've been chasing you since Egypt."

"Indeed? Why is that?"

"Well, see," Jack said, pacing a bit on the upper deck. "You've got a couple things of ours, and we need 'em back."

Ecke strode to the middle of the lower deck and stood alone with his arms out in a gesture of openness. "I'm sure I don't know what you mean," he chimed innocently.

"Let's cut the bullshit," Doc scolded. "We want our dynamo and our engineer, and we'll be out of your way."

Jack cringed at Doc's use of common cowboy language, but she was impressive nonetheless.

Ecke sighed. "Alas, you are too late, on both counts."

Doc and Jack exchanged a desperate look.

"You see," Ecke continued, "Your engineer destroyed the dynamo rather than show us its workings."

Jack squinted down at the man. He wasn't sure whether to believe it. "Good boy, Rivets," said Jack after a few seconds of confusion. "So where is he, anyway?"

Ecke caught himself looking down at the floor. "Because he was of no further use to us, Maria Blutig was to sacrifice him for the ritual tonight on the beach."

Doc found herself instantly furious. Pulling the sidearm from her own uniform holster, she pointed it at Ecke. "Okay, then, you're coming with us."

"One moment, my dear," Ecke said, just as Jack spied the navigation officer taking aim with her pistol.

Jack spun, the Colt leading his outstretched arm. "Don't."

Startled, the navigation officer dropped her weapon and showed Jack her empty hands. Doc waved Captain Ecke up the stairs to the upper deck with her pistol.

"We're gonna let your captain show us the way to some transportation," Jack said. "You lot stay put and don't do anything stupid, and I'll tell him where we hid the explosives."

Ecke blinked in surprise. "Explosives?"

Jack grinned as the old man arrived on the upper deck and stood face to face with him. "Of course. You can't build another one of these monster ships without us trying our hand at blowing it up." He pulled the captain's sidearm from its holster and stuffed it in his satchel, then marched Ecke from the bridge.

- CHAPTER 22 -

Jack and Doc had marched Captain Ecke up the stairwell to the topmost gantry when the ship's general quarters alarm began to sound. Spinning red lanterns and klaxon bells cycled in an endless pattern. Jack pressed the muzzle of his Colt into Ecke's spine. "What is this?"

"The ship has gone to general quarters," the old captain explained. "The shore party is finished and we'll be casting off soon."

"Keep going," Doc urged. "We need to get aft to the hangar deck."

"Just play it calm, cool and collected," Jack ordered. "We speak enough German to know if you say anything out of line."

"Ich verstehe," Ecke answered, unfazed. "I understand."

They continued under the spine of the carrier to the aftermost stairwell, and by chance ran into a group of four airmen heading forward in the opposite direction. Each saluted Ecke as he passed along the gantry. One happened to glance down and notice the nickel-plated Colt being pressed into the small of the captain's back. As he passed the trio heading to the stairwell, the airman drew his sidearm and spun to fire at Jack and Doc from behind.

"Halt!" the airman screeched, brandishing his Luger pistol at them. The other airmen, confused at first, followed suit. *"Was passiert hier?"*

As Doc turned to face the men, a shot echoed through the hall, sharp and loud. She felt the air around her left arm expand like a giant balloon, and heard the ripple of space as it absorbed the airman's bullet with a spasm of iridescent light. The slug fell harmlessly to the metal deck.

Another shot flashed from Ecke's left side, and the airman's pistol skittered away down the gantry. The airman grasped his wrist and looked up in surprise. A second Colt peeked around his captain's waist. The towering, chiseled man behind Ecke looked at the airman with impossibly blue eyes and offered a wink.

"*Nein!*" Ecke protested. "Check the envelope for explosives! Go quickly!"

The airmen scattered forward down the gantry, and Jack pushed Ecke toward the stairwell.

"Nicely done, Captain," Jack groused as he followed Ecke up the metal stairs. "You gambled I wouldn't shoot you in the back."

Ecke smiled to himself. "I know your reputation from the war, *Mein Kapitän*. You are a man of honor. It was not such a gamble."

They emerged at the top of the stairwell in the aft section of the aircraft hangar bay. The main door was still open, and would remain so as long as the away party was still ferrying soldiers back from the beach. Jack and Doc had no clue how few Silver Star soldiers would be returning.

The deck officer noticed the arrival of the two commandos from earlier, and the addition of Captain Ecke. The captain wasn't usually bothered with the goings-on of the flight hangar unless something was wrong, so the deck officer moved forward from his desk to see what was the matter.

"*Mein Kapitän?*"

Ecke and Jack both responded with a look, and the deck officer instantly knew things were amiss. Ecke tried to wave him off with a casual, "*Es ist nichts.*" *It's nothing.* But the deck officer had already bolted for the intercom on the wall by his workstation.

Jack pressed the Colt into Ecke's spine and urged him toward the open door to the runway as the deck officer sounded an alarm. Now a secondary klaxon competed with general quarters, creating a cacophony of bells and spinning lights.

"*Schneller,*" Jack grunted.

Doc ran behind the starboard wall of the hangar bay where they'd dumped their gyro-packs. Both were gone. "Jack?" she hollered over the clanging of bells. "The packs are—"

"The packs are safely in our possession," said the commando who stepped through the side door hatch, Luger trained on Doc. A scar ran from his scalp to his chin on the left side, and cold hazel eyes stared at her intently.

Jack and Ecke turned from their position near the fighter plane on the tarmac, surprise written on their faces.

Doc sighed, her shoulders sagging in defeat. "Well...shit."

CR

Duke was almost completely sure the *Daedalus* was firing on the fighter planes and not the gyro pilots. *Almost* completely. He became *completely* sure when the *Daedalus* screamed past at full speed, both nose and dorsal turrets spitting red tracer fire into the night sky.

He throttled back a bit and pulled up to watch as the light recon airship, the jewel of the AEGIS Aeronautics division, sent one fighter, then a second, spiraling into the tropical jungle in a burst of flames. Cipher and Ace pulled up at his flanks and Duke realized they'd been in the sky for quite some time. They'd done their job as a screen for Silver Star air support, and now they needed to meet up with the land contingent. He was fairly sure they'd find Nemo and the rest over on the west side of the island, somewhere around Fort Sanctuary. He gestured west and angled away, Cipher and Ace hot on his tail.

Out of the corner of his eye, he caught a blast of red tracer fire and the third fighter arced into the air, trailing bright orange flames. The screams of the pilot were audible for a short moment before the fuel tank exploded and the whole frame dropped like a rock.

That was six fighters accounted for, the entire compliment from the *Osiris.*

They'd only encountered the six aircraft. The *Luftpanzer* carried three more.

"Heads up," Duke shouted at his wingmen. "There are still potentially three more, somewhere."

With one eye scanning the moonless night for signs of the other fighter planes, they descended over the jungle on a westerly heading, and within minutes found themselves hovering over what looked and sounded like a pitched firefight in the jungle below. The rapid *pops* and typewriter rhythms of automatic weapons echoed up through the canopy and between the volcanic mountains. The harsh white glow of battle flares was punctuated by flashes of muzzle fire.

Duke found a suitable clearing and waved Cipher and Ace to follow. He throttled back and descended into the roiling jungle, coming down in the middle of a vine-covered trail. The smoldering uniforms of Silver Star commandos were strewn across the ground into the thick brush, where others who were still alive had taken cover, shooting at another group across the clearing, behind a mossy outcropping of volcanic rock. As he landed, he felt the full weight of the gyro-pack come down on his back and he lost his footing, stumbling backward onto the rocks. One of the rotor blades snapped off on impact, and he realized he was wide open, facing the group in the underbrush.

Forcing the right control arm into a roughly lateral position, he squeezed the trigger and emptied the sixty-round drum of ammo, covering Cipher and Ace as they descended into the same clearing, but further behind his position and out of direct fire.

Cipher came down fast, and because she was favoring her left leg, toppled over to the right, shearing off both rotor blades and falling in an unconscious heap.

Ace throttled down slowly, landing lightly on a trail rise about fifty yards behind the outcropping. He immediately shrugged out of the harness and ditched the pack, pulling a black revolver from his side holster and heading for cover as he scanned the dim clearing for his comrades. He found Cipher and pulled her off the trail into a cascade of tropical vines and broad-leaf palms.

The jungle was quiet for a moment after the smoke cleared from the Tommy gun's barrel, and Duke lay back, still strapped into the pack, panting and sweaty. His right arm throbbed and he couldn't see out of his left eye. With a trembling left hand, he reached up and removed the muddy goggles, rectifying his vision problem.

Immediately the clearing was full of gunfire again, and Duke curled into a fetal position to present as small a target a possible, perhaps forgetting he was strapped to an eighty-pound flying contraption and splayed out on a large rock with no cover.

This time some of the gunfire was answered from behind the rocks, and Duke glanced up to see a huge looming shape over him on the outcropping above. It was a good six feet tall and simian in build. But most gorillas Duke had seen, in zoos and on safaris, didn't shoot submachine guns while shouting curses—in English.

The gorilla stood on its flat, hand-like feet, emptying the entire drum magazine from an MP-18 into the brush, and Duke thought it was simultaneously the most ridiculous and most inspiring sight he'd ever seen.

Other people began to emerge from behind the rocks, firing at positions in the brush. Someone popped another white flare above the canopy, lighting up the clearing with a macabre spider's web of veiny shadows as it descended on its parachute.

Duke struggled to free himself from the pack harness, but the locking mechanism was stuck. He watched the exchange of fire between the rocks and the brush, trying to wriggle from his prone position on the rocks.

Suddenly all went silent for a brief second, and the trees began to sway and shudder violently. A chilling, alien call went up into the jungle canopy, and then the brush was full of screams as the eldritch monstrosities dropped on them. Duke's eyes widened as unearthly animal growls merged with the anguish of men being ripped apart while still alive. He struggled even more forcefully this time, managing to roll the pack over so that he was underneath. But then he heard the grinding click of claws on pumice, and he looked up to behold the face of horror. The thing looked back at him through its arachnoid eyes, and Duke suddenly felt very weak. His willpower began to drain, and he couldn't look away. He felt his consciousness, his very life force being pulled from him. The shriek of agony from every fiber of his being filled his skull with a deafening roar, and his vision began to tunnel inward. Blackness washed over him.

A shot rang out, followed by two more. Pieces of the demon exploded across the rocks, spattering the soft moss in black ichor. Deadeye stepped down from the outcropping, racking another round into his Winchester carbine. He shot from the hip, pulverizing the creatures where they stood. Some were sluggish from feeding on Silver Star commandos. They were the first to die. Nemo and her sailors then stepped into the clearing, firing their gyrojet guns and slashing with cutlasses.

Kate Shakespeare stood atop the rocks and supplied covering fire from her rifle, while the gorilla Nariaal replaced the drum magazine on his submachine gun.

The horrors that hadn't fed were quick enough to escape the barrage, leaping and skittering into the jungle like dog-sized spiders.

Deadeye rounded up his troops as Nemo's unit searched the bushes to find only shredded uniforms and piles of ash among the smoldering carcasses of a handful of demonic creatures. Neela found Ace and Cipher near the trail and arranged first aid for the unconscious aeronaut. Nemo's medic, a young Chinese woman, cut Duke from his harness and looked him over.

"How is he?" Deadeye asked.

"Alive," she answered, "but he is unresponsive. He will need more medical care than we can give him here."

"Make a litter," Nariaal ordered. "We will carry him. And the woman," he added, pointing at the trail where Neela was tending the unconscious Cipher.

Nemo emerged from the brush and sheathed her cutlass in a scabbard on her left hip. "Nariaal, where do we go now? The soldiers seem to be on the run."

"We follow them to the western shore," answered the ape-man. "And we keep fighting. Until none of the Silver Star remain."

The commando popped off a shot with the Luger, and once again Doc felt the world stop around her, as if suspended in gelatin. The slug slowed and dropped to the deck with a *tink!* The commando fired again—a shot that ordinarily would have hit her in the chest— and the space around her bubbled and warped with a flash of iridescence.

Without turning, she backed toward the fighter plane and Jack as he held his own gun on Ecke. Another shot slowed and dropped to the tarmac. Jack held the Colt in his left hand at the small of Ecke's back as he fired a couple shots with his right, and Ecke covered his ears.

Realizing that he wasn't going to hit Doc due to whatever mystical force of protection she was invoking, and he couldn't hit Jack without risking hitting his captain, the commando ducked back inside the hatch and disappeared.

"Jack," warned Doc, "you do know this plane is a single-seater?"

"I do," he said, turning to Ecke. "Captain, it's been a pleasure. You will understand if we borrow your plane?"

"Yes, Captain," Ecke replied, stepping cautiously back as Jack fished his flight cap and goggles from his satchel.

Doc wasn't sure what the plan was, but she followed suit. As Jack helped her onto the right lower wing, she realized that he expected her to ride on it. "Are you kidding me?" she gasped.

Jack grabbed her shoulders and touched his forehead to hers. "I know you can do this. It's gonna be a short trip. I just need you to hang on and trust me." He did a quick circuit around the plane, untying the wheels from the deck cleats, then climbed into the cockpit and thumbed on the ignition. The engine sputtered and coughed what sounded like a gunshot into the air as it cranked to life, the propeller spinning up instantly.

Ecke watched them from a short distance away. "Where are the explosives?" he shouted.

When Jack was sure Doc was in a solid position laying flat against the right side of the fuselage, arms threaded through the innermost support frame, he turned to the bearded officer and glanced at his watch. "Starboard ballonets. You have about six minutes, Captain. If I were you, I'd find a way off this ship."

The plane rolled forward at slower than normal takeoff speed. The runway was already a couple hundred feet up, and Jack didn't want to push it with Doc hanging into the outside. The wheels left the nose end of the tarmac, and the plane dropped at first, but Jack gave it some throttle and pulled up on the stick. They leveled out, made a leisurely turn and looked for a place to land, or at least crash with minimal loss of life and limb.

The beach had been abandoned. Brazier fires still flickered in the wan pink light of false dawn. Crumpled acolyte robes and soldier fatigues lay strewn randomly across the beach. The gyro skiff was gone, along with all of the important hardware from Himmler's experiment. As they watched from above, the door in the picket wall thrust open, and a cadre of humans and beast folk stormed onto the beach. An elated cry went up from the holding pen, where the original beast folk sacrifices had been locked. They were rapidly set freey.

Jack saw someone on the beach take aim with a rifle, and he waggled his wings to signal friendliness. Deadeye approached Kate and said something while guiding her weapon down.

"There's nowhere to make a safe landing on the island," Jack shouted above the roar of the plane engine. "I don't want to risk you getting hurt, so I'm gonna do a soft water landing."

Doc nodded, her eyes tired through the goggles. "Do what you gotta do."

Suddenly the plane lit up with flashes of green, and the two missing planes dived down on him. He couldn't risk much in the way of evasive action without endangering Doc's life. He had to set the plane down on the water, and hope for a shallow swim to shore or a deep water rescue.

The second fighter swooped from above, peppering the stolen HD 23 with green tracer fire. The left lower wing was torn in half, whipping away under the fuselage. Jack fought to throttle down and cut the engine to avoid a fire. A second barrage tore through the tail of the plane and shattered the glass of the altitude gauge, miraculously missing both occupants.

The wind whipped past Doc's face as she braced for impact.

As the fighters circled around to finish them off, Jack eased the stick down, slapping the belly of the plane on the glassy blue-gray surface of the Pacific. Salt spray erupted from the collision, covering Doc in mist. Jack removed his cap and goggles, checking around to get their bearings. They were a good two hundred yards from the western beach. It would be a tough swim.

"Are you okay?" he asked Doc, who was in the process of extracting herself from the right wing brace assembly.

"I'm fine," she said, relieved to hear herself say it.

"They're coming back," he warned. "Think you can swim for it?"

"Doesn't look like we've got a choice."

As the sun tentatively peeked over the eastern horizon in ribbons of pink and gold, two Silver Star fighters began their strafing run. Jack and Doc prepared to leap into the water.

Ducking instinctively at the sound of machine gun fire, they heard several loud cracks and were astonished to see bits of wood and machinery zing past them, peppering the water with debris. Jack turned just in time to see the second fighter nose over and hit the water at 165 miles per hour.

The mammoth body of the *Nautilus* had risen from the depth some fifty yards distant. On the aft deck, one of Nemo's gunnery officers saluted from behind the smoldering barrel of a Browning heavy machine gun.

Doc turned to Jack and smiled as he watched the *Nautilus* crew inflate another rubber raft and begin the rescue operation. "I like our new friends," she said.

Jack chuckled. Glancing up into the Pacific morning sky, he noted that in the minutes since their departure, the *Luftpanzer* had cut loose its mooring cable and disappeared. He kept an ear out, listening for the sound of an explosion that never came.

- CHAPTER 23 -

Cipher and Duke were transferred aboard the *Daedalus* and flown back to Nemo's stronghold on Tabor Island. Jack and Doc represented AEGIS in their first contact with the beast folk of Sanctuary, and were gratified when the animal hybrids welcomed them. Neela was reunited with her father, the Sayer of the Law, as he was freed from the stockade.

The Sayer of the Law held an impromptu council meeting on the western beach, and it was decided that the demons summoned by the Silver Star that had escaped into the jungle must be eradicated, although it certainly appeared they lacked a taste for beast folk. They were still dangerous, and if the Kanak people ever returned to the north shore, they would be at risk. Doc would take one of the carcasses back with her to the home office in West Orange, New Jersey, for further study.

AEGIS would be allowed to send scientists and soldiers to teach the beast folk of Sanctuary how to better protect themselves as the world continued to become smaller in size through exploration and technology.

A representative from Sanctuary would go with the airship crews to learn and study. A collective sob rushed through the gathered Sanctuary natives when Nariaal volunteered to be that representative. "It should be me," he insisted when Nemo asked if he were sure. "I have learned all I can at the House of Pain. My mind craves more."

Rivets was reunited with his crewmates, and introduced to Sparks, the young Kenyan engineer. She impressed him. Like Deadeye, Jack and Doc were shocked at Rivets' physical decline. He had clearly suffered at the hands of the Silver Star, and a guilt set in to Doc that would follow her for a long time. She had recruited him into the organization after all, drawing from a cadre who had served together in the war. At least he'd be back home soon and recovering under her care, which assuaged the guilt somewhat. As the *Nautilus* sat at anchor off the beach and the boats were readied for the return trip, Rivets took Jack and Doc aside.

"I know what you went through to find me," he growled. "And I love you both for doin' it."

Doc smiled sadly. "But...?"

"I think I'm gonna stay put for awhile. Help these folks get some of the basics set up—runnin' water and the like."

Jack cracked a half smile and rubbed his jaw. "I dunno, Rivets. Stuck out here on a tropical paradise with a bunch of..."

"Beast folk. They're a-okay by me, Jack. And I owe one o' them my life."

There was no talking him out of it. Try as he might, Jack couldn't conceive of a good reason to keep him from staying there. He would be an asset to the natives, and when AEGIS arrived with more personnel, he'd be a great point of contact. Besides, with Sparks aboard, their engine room was in more than capable hands.

It was agreed that the crews of the *Percival* and *Daedalus* would make no official report regarding Nemo, her submarine, or her base on Tabor. In return, Nemo would be much more selective in her choice of targets, and considered laying off Allied shipping altogether. There were still plenty of pirates in the Pacific and Indian Oceans to pick on.

Radio detector scans tracked the *Osiris* and *Luftpanzer,* or two large aircraft they assumed were the supercarriers, back into the Asian region where they disappeared from the scopes altogether. Whatever their project had been, the results and the participants had disappeared with the giant ships.

The two airship crews said their farewells and set course for Lima, Peru, just over two thousand miles east. Three days after the *Daedalus* and *Percival* departed, the apparition of a tall, pale woman began to appear on the western shore of Sanctuary at night. Beast folk were not permitted beyond the picket wall after dark, until AEGIS sent someone to investigate.

During the journey, Nariaal spent much of his free time studying every inch of structure, envelope, and console. He and Sparks compared notes over strong coffee and long games of Bao, a Kenyan variant of Mancala. In Lima they were informed that the AEGIS field office in London had made a special request to meet with, and perhaps recruit, Nariaal for a special assignment. Doc phoned long distance to have her aunts bring Ellen to London to meet them. A fast steamer from New York would make Southampton in just under five days. The flight plan from Lima to London shook out to a little over sixty-one hours at their new cruising speed. Jack and Doc would be reunited with their daughter in less than a week.

The return of the *Percival* and her sister ship *Daedalus* was headline news all over Britain. Newsreel film crews mobbed the airfield at RAF Cardington as the two dirigibles arrived and were towed to the giant hangar facility.

Colonel Stephen Shaw, AEGIS London bureau chief, met the ships, debriefed the crews, and arranged for Nariaal to be escorted away in secret, while Jack and the other non-gorilla agents agreed to media interviews as a cover for his escape. The aeronauts dispersed on their own recognizance until further notice, having received a generous stipend that more than covered their hotel and meals. They were to remain within twenty-four hours travel time from London.

Duke received specialized care from a neuro-scientist at London Hospital. He came out of his coma two days after arriving, and was slow to rebound. Something had left an indelible mark on his very soul. Ace stayed at Cipher's bedside until she was fully recovered. She healed quickly, and was off crutches in a week.

Deadeye and Kate Shakespeare began a whirlwind romance that began in London, wound through Scotland, and ended up in a posh Paris hotel. Charlie hadn't actually seen the City of Lights since the war, so he made sure to show her all the old hangouts.

Barrett, Mahmoud, Fraser, and Farmingham all signed up for AEGIS special training, which took them to a former RAF base in Wales for six weeks of quiet study. It was heaven in comparison to baking in the dry heat of the Egyptian desert, sweating in the wet heat of the South Pacific, or getting shot at by agents of the Silver Star.

Jack and Doc spent a luxurious week at the Sheraton on Park Lane, sleeping in a great, soft bed on clean sheets, dining in the opulent Art Deco restaurant, and generally making up for lots of lost sleep and deferred lovemaking. When Aunts Mille and Agnes arrived with Ellen in tow, a new phase of extended celebration was initiated. Trips to the London Zoo and British Museum, shopping at Harrod's, and boat rides down the Thames, the paparazzi never far away. Ellen was used to having famous parents, and she now felt like she was a part of that fame.

After a couple of weeks of family fun, Agnes and Millie returned to the States, and Ellen continued on with her parents. About the same time, Colonel Shaw telephoned the hotel room to invite them to a special meeting between AEGIS and the British military.

The military intelligence vetting process was a complete about-face from the London holiday they'd been enjoying, but they made it through with a lot of shrugs and shared laughter. It could have been worse, but for Colonel Shaw vouching for the three of them whenever some new department head muscled his or her way in for more questions.

They were finally blindfolded and put in a car for an hour's drive to a secret location outside London. Once there, they were led inside an underground facility, which had originally been a bomb shelter during the war, or so they were told. Whatever its origin, it had since been expanded, to say the least. The concrete bunker was vast, with a curved ceiling that ran the length of the entire place. Jack was almost sure they could have fit both the *Luftpanzer* and *Osiris* down there.

Jack, Doc, and Ellen strolled along the endless concrete hallway, watching as various men and women in British Army uniforms or white lab coats made their way to and from important work. Shaw leaned over to Doc as they strolled. "You mentioned the experiment on the island seems to have been a demonic summoning of sorts?"

"That's what it looked like," Doc nodded.

Shaw pursed his lips. "There's been talk that a Russian scientist has perfected a method for trapping a demonic entity in a machine of sorts, as a power source."

Jack squinted, stopping the group as they conversed. "This Silver Star project appeared to be all German and British or American. I've never run across any Russians working with the Silver Star."

"Whatever it is they're up to," Shaw said ominously, "we need to be ready for it."

Ellen stared up at the adults as they whispered, silently vowing she'd eventually find out secrets on her own. She'd be a professional secret-finder-outer.

A familiar figure appeared—the giant silverback gorilla with gleaming eyes. He was clad in a white lab smock that buttoned up both sides of his chest, but still padded on those wide, unshod feet. He clutched a clipboard in a massive simian hand, and wore a pair of lab goggles atop his broad forehead.

"Ah," Shaw said, "Doctor Nariaal."

Doc and Jack exchanged a look. "Doctor?" they chimed in unison.

Shaw laughed. "Oh, yes, when we tested our friend here, his results were off every chart. He was awarded multiple graduate degrees from Cambridge."

The gorilla nodded. "The title is honorary as yet. My doctoral thesis is still in progress."

Ellen realized they were standing next to a talking gorilla scientist, and under her breath proclaimed it the Best Day Ever.

Jack smiled, fishing a new pack of gum from his jacket pocket. "I take it you didn't call us all the way out here just for a reunion, Colonel."

Shaw glanced at the ground, then at each member of the group. The scar behind his eye patch flexed and wrinkled in the sickly, off-yellow fluorescent lighting. "Indeed not, Captain." He explained that a colossal secret had been kept from the world. A secret Britain could no longer keep, in the face of the rising challenge to freedom and democracy from groups like the Silver Star and the increasingly brazen fascist states of Europe.

As Nariaal led them through a side hall and down another long corridor to a guarded warehouse where everyone had to sign in, Shaw cleared his throat nervously. "Something happened to Britain at the end of the last century. A terrible event befell our island nation, which we managed to keep secret from the rest of the world. We're still studying the aftermath, and have been for the past three decades." They entered the warehouse through a solid metal door, and lights flickered on, first nearby, then into the distance.

Here there was mechanical wreckage on a scale Jack hadn't experienced since the war. In fact, it dwarfed most battles he'd seen from the sky. Strange engines of unknown configurations littered the place. Bits of armor shell and weird bio-mechanical structures protruded from armatures bigger than the thrust engines on the *Daedalus*. In the middle of it all sat what looked like a giant copper housing about twenty feet in diameter, like two pot lids stuck together at the rims. A complex armature and some wires were hidden beneath. To the side, a long, slender, articulated mechanical leg, made from the same copper-like material, arched gracefully in an inverted V. Jack could see two other legs crushed beneath the massive saucer-shaped frame. It had once been a tripod machine of some sort, unless he missed his guess. All of the metal cladding was covered in a strange script Jack wasn't familiar with.

Doc's mouth fell open as she looked over the inscriptions on the copper constructions and realized they were similar, though not identical, to the cuneiform writing of an ancient eldritch language utilized in dark magic rituals throughout centuries past. Used in summoning ancient terrors from across time and space. Used currently by people like Crowley and the Silver Star.

"Where..." she gasped for breath. "Where did this come from?"

Colonel Shaw paused a moment, glancing at each person as if to swear them to secrecy yet again. He cleared his throat nervously, casting his gaze upward.

"Mars."

The End

ABOUT THE AUTHOR

Todd Downing's love affair with genre fiction dates back to his consumption of classic radio dramas and comic books as a child in the 1970s, which broadened into a general appreciation for scifi and fantasy media of all kinds.

He grew up in the greater San Francisco Bay Area, writing and drawing from a young age, his works ever-present in school literary journals and newspapers, and eventually on film. He married his high school sweetheart and moved to Seattle in 1991 where he began to write professionally, and worked as an artist in the videogame industry until his publishing company became a full time operation, while raising two children amid the chaos.

As the co-founder and creative director of Deep7 Press, Downing is the primary author and designer of over fifty roleplaying titles, including *Arrowflight, Grimmworld, Airship Daedalus*, and the official *Red Dwarf* RPG. He continues to write genre fiction for stage, film, comics, audio, and adventure gaming products.

Widowed to cancer in 2005, Downing remarried in 2009 and currently lives in a three-generation home in Port Orchard, Washington, with his wife, her mother, their daughter, four cats, and a flock of unruly chickens. Thankfully, he has an office with a door that closes.

Join the author's mailing list:
www.todddowning.com

Thrilling pulp adventure!
www.airshipdaedalus.com

Read the adventures of the Airship *Daedalus:*
A Shield Against the Darkness (Book #1)
*Assassins of the
Lost Kingdom* (Book #2, by E.J. Blaine)
The Golden City (Book #3)
Legend of the Savage Isle (Book #4)
The Arctic Menace (Book #5)

Plus:

AEGIS Tales
A Retro-Pulp Anthology, Volume 1

Primordial Soup Kitchen
A Collection of Short Strangeness

Calico Kids

The Parish

AVAILABLE NOW
in ebook and print!